# The Headless Bride

Look for the first exciting title in
THE GHOST IN THE DOLLHOUSE series:

#1 *Dollhouse of the Dead*

# THE GHOST IN THE DOLLHOUSE
## The Headless Bride

### Kathryn Reiss

AN
**APPLE**
PAPERBACK

SCHOLASTIC INC.

New York   Toronto   London   Auckland   Sydney

No part of this publication may be reproduced in whole or in part, or stored in a retrieval system, or transmitted in any form or by any means, electronic, mechanical, photocopying, recording, or otherwise, without written permission of the publisher. For information regarding permission, write to Scholastic Inc., 555 Broadway, New York, NY 10012.

ISBN 0-590-60361-2

12 11 10 9 8 7 6 5 4 3 2 1          7 8 9/9 0 1 2/0

Printed in the U.S.A.          40
First Scholastic printing, April 1997

*This book is for our son
Daniel Geoffrey,
who can read it all by himself.*

# The Headless Bride

# Chapter 1

There was a ghost in Zibby Thorne's dollhouse. *And you'd think,* Zibby frowned as she laboriously glued a little picture of an apple pie into a tiny wooden frame, *that if a girl is nice enough to let a ghost live in her doll-house, that ghost could at least be grateful.* But, far from expressing gratitude, the ghost in Zibby's dollhouse was becoming more and more demanding by the day. And Zibby was getting tired of it.

*Oh, Zibby, Zibby!* wailed the little voice in her head. It was the voice of the ghost of Primrose Parson, who had once been a ninety-year-old woman, but was now a spirit who chose to inhabit the little dollhouse doll with the brown braids and the fancy blue dress. Zibby's best friend, Jude Jefferson, liked to say that Primrose was enjoying a second childhood at Zibby's expense. Jude kept telling Zibby simply to ignore Primrose. But Jude didn't know how it felt to have a ghostly voice whining right inside her head. And ignoring Primrose was impossible.

1

*Zibby, isn't the picture ready yet? The walls in here are really too awfully bare! I can't stand these barren walls another second!*

"Hang on a sec," said Zibby in as soothing a voice as she could manage. "I'm waiting for the glue to dry." She ran her fingers through her chin-length red-gold hair as if to scrub the little voice out of her head. Then she looked over at Jude, Penny, and Charlotte. It wasn't fair that they weren't being haunted, too.

"What did she say?" asked Jude Jefferson from her place on the floor where she was gluing tiny strips of balsa wood together.

"You get one guess," Zibby said morosely.

"More complaints?" asked Penny Jefferson.

"What else?" Zibby sighed. "She wants us to hurry up. She can't bear the bare walls."

"Can't *bear* the *bare* walls!" giggled Penny. "She's probably just making a joke. I think you're too hard on her, Zibby."

Zibby glowered at her. Penny was always trying to look on the bright side of every situation, which sometimes got on Zibby's nerves. Surprisingly, the only one of the girls who really seemed to understand how difficult life with the ghost had become was Zibby's cousin, Charlotte Wheeler. Zibby and Charlotte had never been especially close, but since they'd discovered the ghost, Charlotte had been easier to bear.

"I think the ghost is horrible," Charlotte commiserated now, flipping back the long blonde hair she spent so much time brushing and styling. "Poor Zibby. I don't know how you stand it. I'd hate to have ghosts at my house." She was sitting on Zibby's bed cutting little pictures out of one of Zibby's mom's food magazines. The little pictures of elegant food would be framed to dress up the dollhouse walls.

"But she's not as horrible as Miss Honeywell was," Penny reminded them.

There had once been another ghost in Zibby's dollhouse, but Zibby tried hard not to think about that.

The four girls had an assembly line going now, all because Primrose Parson needed artwork on her dollhouse walls. Charlotte chose the pictures and cut them out. Jude snipped the tips off wooden matchsticks and trimmed them to fit the pictures. Then she glued the sticks together to make tiny frames. When they were dry, Penny stained the wood with colored felt-tip pens. Last of all, Zibby glued the little pictures into the frames. So far they had five framed pictures ready to hang. Zibby thought they looked nice. Bottles of wine, ripe veiny cheeses, a basket with eggs inside, a luscious-looking chocolate cake, and now the apple pie. The pictures were making Zibby hungry.

The doll in the blue dress lay on the tiny couch in the downstairs parlor of the big dollhouse. The room was furnished partly with tiny, exquisitely crafted furniture that had come with the dollhouse, and partly

with things Zibby and her friends had provided —
sprigs of dried flowers planted in toothpaste caps, a rug
made from a tightly woven drinks coaster that Penny
had donated, and curtains made from Charlotte's fancy
lace handkerchief. Charlotte liked elegant things. The
other girls found her sophisticated act hard to take,
sometimes, but she did tend to have all sorts of baubles
and bits in her bedroom that proved useful in meeting
the ghost's demands.

Dolefully, Zibby accepted the last little frame from
Penny, this one colored green, and searched for a picture to fit inside it. Primrose had been nagging for
weeks, and finally the girls gave in. As if Zibby didn't
have enough going on already, with her mom getting
married in a few days! It wasn't fair that she should
have to sit in her room on a beautiful summer's day,
hard at work like this, when there were so many things
she could be doing to help with the wedding.

In fact, she was supposed to be getting ready to go
out with her mom and Ned for dinner. Zibby liked
Ned Shimizu a lot, but tried not to think too much
about his two kids, Laura-Jane and Brady. She would
be living with them some of the time, and hardly knew
them. But what she knew, she didn't like much. So they
were all going out to dinner tonight to get used to each
other.

*Zibby, Zibby! Hurry up!* came Primrose's imperious
voice.

4

"Hold your horses," Zibby snapped. "We're working as fast as we can."

*Horses are another thing I've been meaning to speak to you about. I'd like a carriage and a team of horses to pull it — oh, I know you can't get tiny horses, but you could train some hamsters —*

"Shut up, Primrose." Zibby had lost all patience.

*What a rude child you are,* replied Primrose in an injured tone. Her little voice was silent inside Zibby's head for a moment and Zibby relaxed, thinking the ghost would leave her in peace for a while, but Primrose's voice returned. This time it sounded haughty.

*I've decided I don't like all these pictures of food, so you can just take them all away and start again,* Primrose's voice announced inside Zibby's head. *Ghosts can't eat food, you know, but we can remember food. It's cruel of you to make me look at all these cakes and pies and things. And besides, pictures of food aren't real art. I want art.*

Zibby threw down the little frame she had been holding. It fell onto her desk, on top of the newest postcard from her dad, who lived in Italy with his second wife. "I'm sick and tired of you, Primrose Parson!" she growled. "Now you just hush up, or you can forget about getting any paintings at all!"

"Uh-oh, Zibby, what's she doing now?" asked Jude, frowning.

"Complaining, of course." Zibby picked up the postcard and looked at the picture. It was a landscape shot of fields and an old church. Zibby hadn't seen her dad in almost two years, but he wrote regularly, one postcard each week, and Zibby had a whole stack of cards in a shoe box on her desk.

*Now that's what I call art, Zibby. I want it for the dining room.*

"And cover the whole wall, practically?" muttered Zibby. "The postcard is way too big."

*Not the card, silly girl. I want the* stamp *from the card. Now that's real artwork. Not like the silly pictures your cousin is cutting out from those magazines! You can frame all those stamps from your cards, instead.*

Zibby flipped the card over and looked at the stamp. It showed a sketch of a stone statue — a winged gargoyle, no doubt from some building in Italy. Next Zibby rifled through the box of postcards, studying the stamps. There were pictures of castles, animals, reproductions of famous paintings, portraits of famous Italian people.

*I* insist *that you frame these stamps instead,* Primrose directed her haughtily. *Immediately!*

In life Primrose Parson had been a rich little girl. She had had servants and indulgent parents. She had been used to getting her own way in most things. She had grown to be an old woman, and considered herself very wise. Although her ghost chose to inhabit the little girl doll, the spirit itself was old. Primrose Parson saw no reason why young girls should not obey her instantly, as she believed children should when adults gave orders.

"Forget it!" Zibby snapped. Jude, Penny, and Charlotte looked up from their work, perplexed. "You're a bossy little ghost, Primrose Parson, but you're forgetting one thing." Zibby's voice rose angrily. She forgot she was dealing with a ghost. She spoke as she would to a rude child. "This is *my* dollhouse! You are a guest. And guests can be turned out — if they aren't polite and on their best behavior."

*Are you threatening me?* came Primrose's reedy voice in Zibby's head. *I certainly hope you aren't. I don't like being threatened.*

"What's she saying?" asked Jude. "Zibby, what's wrong?"

"Come hear this for yourself." Zibby held out her hands and Jude and Penny reached over and clasped them. Charlotte jumped off the bed and moved in between Jude and Penny. The girls had discovered soon after the ghost appeared that while she spoke only in Zibby's head, the others could hear her, too, if they were physically connected to Zibby. So the four of them stood in a circle in Zibby's room, hands linked to hands.

"I'm not threatening you," Zibby explained slowly. "But I'm *warning* you. You need to have better manners. You need to appreciate what we've done for you. We've been working hard this afternoon, making pictures for your walls, and now you're suddenly saying you don't like them and want different pictures instead. Well, that's just too bad."

"What pictures does she want now?" asked Penny.

"The stamps off my postcards," Zibby replied tersely. "She says they're more like real artwork. She says she doesn't like pictures of food because she can't eat food anymore."

*Cruel!* whispered Primrose Parson's voice through their heads. *So cruel.*

Jude jumped, startled at this sign of the ghost. She tried to pull her hand away, but Zibby held tight. Charlotte flinched, looking pale. She, more than any of the others, feared ghosts.

"Well, we could change them, I suppose," began Penny in a determinedly cheerful voice. "I wouldn't like it if people hung stuff on the walls in my room that I didn't like. Poor Primrose!"

"Poor Primrose, nothing!" Zibby wasn't feeling so obliging. Being haunted by the ghost this summer had worn down her nerves. Never knowing when the ghost would speak kept Zibby on edge.

*Get busy, little girls,* instructed Primrose's high-pitched voice. *I'm waiting.*

"Yeah, and you can keep on waiting," muttered Zibby.

*You're an ill-bred, stupid child!*

"Nya, nya, sticks and stones," returned Zibby. "I'm surprised a grown-up ghost like you would stoop to

8

name-calling! Talk about bad manners. I don't want you here anymore, Primrose Parson. You're just making trouble." She sniggered unkindly. "And if you weren't dead already, I'd happily kill you!"

There was a silence, as if Primrose were shocked. Jude tightened her hold on Zibby's hand. But the silence did not last long. *Last chance,* came the ghost's reply.

"Maybe we'd better do what she wants," whispered Charlotte fearfully. "I mean —"

"No." Zibby's voice was firm. "If she's going to live in the dollhouse, it's got to be on my terms, don't you see? Otherwise, she's just going to keep bothering me all the time!"

"Don't forget," said Jude softly, "you don't have a lot of choice in the matter."

Trust practical Jude to point that out. Zibby frowned at her friend. "I *do* have a choice! I can close up the dollhouse. Lock it up. And put it in the basement." If the house were closed and locked, the ghost was trapped and her voice silenced.

*Just try it!* Primrose's unpleasant chuckle resounded in all their heads. *Go ahead and try!*

"All right, I will." Zibby dropped Jude's and Penny's hands and crossed the bedroom to the dollhouse. It was an old wooden house almost three feet high, built as a tall box with a peaked roof and a hinged front that opened double panels out from the middle and closed with a latch. Normally Zibby kept the two front panels open so that the rooms inside were revealed. There were eight rooms, four on the ground floor, four upstairs, and an attic. Now she slammed the front walls shut and flicked the latch into place. "There!"

Primrose's unpleasant chuckle sounded again in her head. Zibby peered in through the parlor window and could see the little girl doll in the blue dress still seated on the couch. How could she still hear Primrose's voice if the house were latched shut? Zibby had understood that the magic had its limits. That's what the ghost had told her.

Charlotte sat down on the bed, looking miserable. Penny stood watching the house with wide brown eyes. Jude came over to Zibby and put her hand on Zibby's arm. "Is she locked in?"

Because Jude's hand was on Zibby's arm, both girls were able to hear the little voice when it spoke. *You're not going to trap me! But I can take a hint. I know when I'm not wanted. If you don't want me, I'll go! You can let Miss Honeywell live here, for all I care.* And the ghostly little chuckle faded into a sob, and then all was quiet.

"Is she gone?" whispered Jude.

"What do you mean, gone?" asked Zibby. "The doll is still in there, so the ghost must be, too." They could both see the little doll through the window. "Right, Primrose?"

There was no answer.

"Zibby?" Her mom's voice called up the stairs. "Come on down, honey. It's time to go!"

10

Zibby jumped up in relief. "Be right down!" Even an evening out with Ned Shimizu's kids was better than staying home with a sullen ghost. But if the dollhouse were locked up, Zibby reassured herself, Primrose wouldn't be able to make her demands anymore. She wouldn't be able to speak to Zibby at all. Would she?

And silence was what Zibby wanted from the ghost. Wasn't it?

# Chapter 2

Zibby's mom, Nell, was waiting in the front hall, arranging her hair, the same red-gold as Zibby's. She peered into the mirror by the door, then turned to smile at her daughter and the other girls as they came down the stairs. "So, how do I look?"

"Like a bride, Aunt Nell," Charlotte said with a smile.

"You look beautiful, Mom," Zibby agreed. She knew it was what her mom wanted to hear. And it was true, Nell did have a sort of glow around her these days. Since her old high school boyfriend, Ned, had moved back to Carroway, she'd been acting like a teenager in love. Zibby found it embarrassing the way they were always hugging and smooching. They'd been dating only a few months when they'd decided they wanted to get married. It seemed awfully sudden to Zibby — but Nell explained that they already knew each other so well from years ago, and had only catching up to do.

Ned had recently been divorced from his wife, who lived in the next town of Fennel Grove. His children, five-year-old Brady and ten-year-old Laura-Jane, lived half the year with their mother and half the year with Ned. Zibby had met the kids only a couple of times since Nell had been dating Ned, and had not been favorably impressed. Brady appeared to be good-natured enough, but seemed to Zibby like a firecracker — always ready to explode into action or giggles or wild shrieking. He made her nervous. Laura-Jane was just the opposite, very quiet and, her father said, shy. But Zibby wasn't so sure Laura-Jane's watchful brooding was shyness. It seemed deeper than that. Zibby didn't like Laura-Jane, but she tried to hide this from Nell who was all excited about the idea of Ned's kids joining the family. She'd always wanted more children, she told Zibby. The wedding was set for Saturday, only three days away.

Zibby and Nell said good-bye to Charlotte, Jude, and Penny. Charlotte mounted her gleaming ten-speed bike and set off for her large home on the other side of town. Jude and Penny started walking down Oaktree Lane. They had moved into the last house by the park earlier in the summer. Zibby and her mom waited outside on the front porch, enjoying the end-of-August weather. The humidity that had plagued Carroway all summer had disappeared, and though the evening was warm, there was a hint of autumn in the brisk breeze that rustled the oak trees.

Ned's dark blue van turned into their driveway and stopped. The big side door slid open and Brady tumbled out, his black eyes snapping with mischief and his round face split with a huge pumpkin grin. His head was topped with wiry black hair standing on end as if cut by a lawn mower. "Hi!" he shrieked to Zibby and Nell. "Do you like pepperoni or sausage better?"

"Or some of both?" said Ned, coming up the path behind his son. "Hello there, ladies. I hope you're hungry because we sure are!" Ned's grin was identical to Brady's, and he exuded a similar warmth and wild energy. He was very different from Zibby's dad, who was thin and tall and quiet, with a shy sideways sort of smile. Zibby's dad didn't smile very often, but when he did, it was as if a light had come on, and his whole face glowed. Nell had always said that Zibby's dad didn't smile enough. He was too serious and grim. "Life isn't so bad," she used to tell him. "Lighten up." Instead of lightening up, he'd gone off to Italy. Zibby wondered if maybe he smiled more there.

Ned was the type who was almost always laughing, the type who made her mom laugh, too.

Zibby watched as Nell ran into Ned's arms and kissed him. Right in public! She looked away in embarrassment. *Really.* Some things should be private.

"Ew! Yuck!" cried Brady, making gagging noises.

Evidently Laura-Jane felt the same. Zibby saw her still in the van, looking out the window, then turning away in disgust. So at least they had *something* in common.

Laura-Jane Shimizu looked very much like her dad and brother, with straight black hair and dark eyes, though her hair was long — almost long enough to sit on, Zibby noticed with envy. Zibby's own hair barely reached past her chin. Laura-Jane wore her hair in two ponytails tied with ribbons. It was a little-girl hairstyle that didn't fit with her sullen expression. It was impossible to tell whether Laura-Jane had the same wide smile as her dad and brother because she never smiled, at least not so Zibby had seen.

"Hey, Brady, calm down," Ned said. "No need to swing from the rafters." He cocked his head at Zibby. "Didn't know that vans had rafters, did you?" Then he grinned at Nell. "What are we standing around here kissing for when there are three hungry children to feed?" Brady tore back to the van, whooping. Ned and Nell followed with hands clasped. Zibby climbed in last and sat next to Laura-Jane.

"Hi," she said.

Laura-Jane muttered something that might have been "hi." She kept looking out the window and didn't say anything to Zibby all the way to the restaurant.

The Pizza Den was packed, even at this early hour. Brady kept pestering his dad for quarters to feed into the video games along the back wall. The two families sat at a large round table near the salad bar. Ned and

Nell sat next to each other and managed to carry on a conversation even though the room was so loud. They ordered two large pizzas — one sausage and one pepperoni.

While they were waiting for the pizza, Ned entertained them by speaking Italian. He tried to teach them the Italian names for things. Zibby listened eagerly. If she wrote her dad a letter in Italian, he would be really impressed.

"Why do we have to speak Italian?" Laura-Jane demanded suddenly.

"Because we're in an Italian restaurant, dummy," said Brady. Then he explained to Zibby. "Dad's always teaching us words in different languages at restaurants. Want to hear me say bathroom in Chinese?"

"No," said Laura-Jane sullenly. So that was something else she and Zibby had in common.

Nell was trying to repeat the different Italian phrases Ned was teaching her. "You're so good with languages," she said admiringly. "I remember you were, even back in high school."

Ned nodded. "I love languages. I'm even taking Japanese lessons now, once a week. It's slow going, though."

"But aren't you Japanese?" asked Zibby.

"Well, my grandparents came from Japan," Ned told her with a smile. "But my parents never learned the language as children, and I never did either. Nor have my kids. Their mom knows some, though."

Laura-Jane flinched at the mention of her mom. She raised her head and stared at her dad with angry eyes. Zibby watched, wondering what the other girl was thinking.

"It's a shame more Americans don't learn foreign languages," Ned was saying.

"I agree," said Nell. "In fact, there are two new caterers in town who specialize in French cooking, and they're both fluent in the language. It's a husband and wife team, and they've lived for years in France, perfecting their techniques and learning the language. I'm afraid I'm going to have some competition now!"

"No one can cook better than you, Mom," Zibby said loyally. Her mom had started selling home-baked food to order shortly before the divorce, but expanded it afterward into a full-time job. Now Nell Thorne ran DaisyCakes, her own catering business. DaisyCakes was immensely popular in Carroway and nearby Fennel Grove — and word had spread. Nell had customers as far afield as Columbus. The food was known for its simple elegance, fresh, organic ingredients, and reasonable prices. *And it's delicious, too*, Zibby thought proudly.

"Who are these new folks?" asked Ned. "Have you met them?"

"Only briefly. They're Hilda and Hector Ballantyne, and I'm meeting them for lunch at the Old Goat tomorrow." The Old Goat was a restaurant down by the river.

"Better brush up on your French," teased Ned.

"Uh-oh," said Nell, and Zibby had to look away again while they smooched.

She sipped her water and thought of the French she was learning in school. French was hard. She tried to imagine being in France and hearing everybody talking like her teacher, Mme. Condé. Then she thought of her dad in Italy. She wanted to visit him there, and meet his Italian wife, Sofia. They would teach her how to speak Italian. She bet it would be easier than French.

The pizzas were brought to their table by a tall, thin boy whose blond thatch of hair fell into his eyes. Brady broke into a cheer when he saw the food and the boy grinned at him.

"Little brothers are a pain," rasped Laura-Jane, slanting a glance up at their waiter, whose nameplate pinned to his rather grubby red and white apron announced that his name was Todd.

"I don't know," replied the boy. "I wouldn't mind one, myself." He hovered by the table as Ned started handing out plates.

Laura-Jane gazed up at the waiter, and a little smile touched her lips. "I'd rather have an *older* brother."

Zibby was relieved to see it was possible for Laura-Jane to smile. The waiter wished them a pleasant meal in a surprisingly deep voice, and walked away. Everyone started eating — except Laura-Jane, who just hunched her shoulders and pecked at the crust. *She looks*, thought Zibby, *like a bird.*

After a while Brady left the table and, having secured a fistful of quarters from his dad, went to the back of the restaurant to play video games. Nell and Ned started talking about their old high school teachers — wondering whether to issue last-minute wedding invitations to the ones who still lived in town. Laura-Jane pushed her plate away and stared into space. After a while she slipped away from the table. Zibby watched her walk back toward the rest rooms. *She walked just like she talked*, Zibby thought. *Quietly. Like a shadow.*

After a while Brady came zooming back to the table, begging for more quarters, snatching the uneaten piece of pizza from his sister's plate, dropping half the cheese topping on the floor as he careened away again. Zibby read the menu over and over and was glad when Ned said it was time to leave, then angry when her mom invited Ned and his kids to come back to their house for some coffee and ice cream. Zibby had had enough of the stony-faced Laura-Jane and her wild-boy brother. She wanted to go home and hang out in her room. She wanted to phone Jude and talk about the fight with Primrose.

But she went back to the house and ate her ice cream at the kitchen table with the others, listening to Ned and Nell reminisce about more people they'd known twenty years before. Brady was busy making bomber noises and throwing bits of scrunched up paper napkins on the floor. Laura-Jane ate her ice cream in tiny snatching bites that made her seem more bird-like than ever, and never spoke above a whisper.

Zibby finished her dessert, but before she could slip away to be by herself, Nell looked up from some old high school yearbooks and asked Zibby to take Laura-Jane and Brady upstairs. "Show them your room, honey, and the attic rooms we'll be fixing up for them."

Ned looked over at Zibby with a smile. "Great idea. We want you kids to get to know each other."

Brady chose to stay at the table, busily waging war with little paper bombs. With a sigh, Zibby obligingly led Laura-Jane upstairs. But she resented the other girl's presence every step of the way.

First Zibby took Laura-Jane up to the attic. There were two small rooms up there, used for storage. Nell had already started emptying things out to make room for the furniture Ned was buying for his children. Ever since Ned had moved to Carroway to work as the features editor of the *Carroway Gazette*, Carroway's daily newspaper, he had been living in the small apartment over the offices. When Laura-Jane and Brady stayed with him, they slept in sleeping bags in the living room. Zibby knew Ned was glad that his children would have more space for themselves once he was living here after the wedding. Zibby was relieved no one had suggested she share a room with Laura-Jane. She didn't think she could bear that.

Laura-Jane looked around the attic, scowling. "The

20

rooms will look nicer when they're painted," Zibby said hastily. She was suddenly aware that the other girl's silence might indicate her horror at the dusty, dark rooms she and her brother were to have. Zibby actually felt sorry for Laura-Jane. "Your dad has already bought the paint, and he and Mom were planning to get everything ready before this weekend. I bet they'll start painting first thing tomorrow so it will all be done by the wedding."

Laura-Jane drew a shaky breath that sounded almost like a sob. "I *hate* that word," she whispered.

"What word?"

"Wedding." Laura-Jane turned away and stomped down the stairs. Zibby followed, frowning. She didn't really mind about the wedding, in fact it was sort of exciting because she and Laura-Jane were going to be bridesmaids. Brady was going to be the ring-bearer, though Zibby privately thought that was a dangerous choice. He would be sure to drop the ring or something.

"You don't want them to get married?" she asked, though it was pretty obvious.

Laura-Jane didn't answer. She just went into Zibby's room and flopped down onto the bed. Zibby sat at her desk, not sure what to say next. It wasn't fair that Nell and Ned had dumped this whispering weirdo on her to entertain while they sat around cooing at each other downstairs.

21

Laura-Jane was looking around Zibby's room. "Oh," she said, her voice slightly louder this time. "You have a dollhouse!"

"Yeah," Zibby said wearily, expecting Laura-Jane to say something about how dumb dollhouses were.

"I have a dollhouse just as big as this one, but mine's just made of plastic," said Laura-Jane. She got up and walked over to stand by Zibby's dollhouse. "This is much nicer."

"Um, you can look at it — but it's better if you don't touch it," Zibby said. She didn't really trust Primrose after their argument. Who knew what sort of mood the ghost was in? She didn't want anything weird to happen in the dollhouse — and freak out Laura-Jane.

Zibby wandered over to the window and looked out at the darkening street. She wished Jude and Penny lived across the street rather than down at the end by the park. If they lived across the street, she could signal them somehow from her bedroom window. They could come over and rescue her from Laura-Jane. Penny's cheerful presence would be especially helpful just now.

Laura-Jane's soft voice made her turn from the window. But Laura-Jane wasn't talking to Zibby. She was kneeling on the floor in front of the dollhouse, murmuring. Was she talking to the ghost?

Zibby knew that had to be impossible, since Laura-

Jane wasn't touching Zibby. Nonetheless, Zibby crossed the room in alarm and stood behind Laura-Jane. "I told you not to touch the dollhouse," Zibby said evenly.

Laura-Jane was holding the father and mother dolls. She ignored Zibby and stood the two dolls up in the hallway. She started humming. The tune she hummed was the wedding march.

"I really don't want anyone playing with it," Zibby said more loudly. She had bought the antique dollhouse at the beginning of the summer. It had come with lots of furniture and a whole sack of a dozen dolls dressed in old-fashioned clothes — and a lot of trouble in the form of an unpleasant ghost. The ghost was not Primrose Parson — *she* had come later — but was Primrose's nasty governess. Miss Honeywell had a streak of evil in her, and had inhabited an old doll dressed in gray — the governess doll. She had terrorized Zibby and her friends by turning their doll-play into real-life tragedies. When they played that Zibby's friend Amy came to visit, Amy and her father were involved in a bad car accident on their way to visit Zibby. When they played that Jude's parents came home from Kenya, the dolls representing the parents accidentally slid off Zibby's bed. But far away in Kenya, Jude's father fell off a cliff. When the mother doll's sleeve had caught on fire, Zibby's own mom had burned her wrist. And poor Charlotte had mysteriously fallen and injured her head after one of the dolls had been toppled into the tiny dollhouse bathtub. There had been more, and all of it unpleasant.

Ever since, even though Miss Honeywell had vanished mysteriously from the dollhouse when the ghost of Primrose Parson moved in, Zibby still felt uneasy playing with the house. The governess doll might reappear at any time, and since Primrose moved in, Zibby hadn't played with the other dolls at all.

"I said not to touch anything," Zibby repeated. She reached for the dolls in Laura-Jane's hands. But Laura-Jane snatched them back.

"Let's play wedding, Zibby. For practice, I mean," said Laura-Jane, with a sly note in her raspy voice that Zibby didn't like at all. "After all, it's only another couple days and we'll be doing it for real." She marched the mother doll down the hallway. "Here comes the bride, all dressed in white." Laura-Jane sang off-key. "Dum, dum-de-dum, dum, dum-de-dum. And here's the groom waiting for her. How touching!"

Zibby reached into the parlor and removed the little girl doll with the brown braids — the Primrose doll. It felt curiously light.

Then she sat, watching with a frown, as Laura-Jane continued her wedding.

"This is the minister," Laura-Jane said, holding up the butler doll. "'Will you take this woman to be your lawfully wedded wife?'" she asked. Then she made the

24

father doll answer. "'I do. I mean, sure, why not? So what if I already have a wife and two kids? What does it matter?'" The butler-minister doll answered, "'Yeah, no problem. You can just ditch them. They don't really count anyway.'"

"Oh, Laura-Jane," said Zibby. "You know that's not the way it is! Your dad and mom are *already* divorced. And so are my parents. And your dad isn't ditching you and Brady — you know he isn't."

Laura-Jane ignored her. She picked up the mother doll and stood her next to the father doll. "'Do you take this man to be your husband?'" she made the butler-minister ask. "'Oh, yes,'" answered the mother doll in a silly, squeaky voice. "'I just love to take away other women's husbands and break up perfectly happy families. It's sort of a hobby of mine.'"

"Shut up!" cried Zibby. "That's not fair!"

Laura-Jane pushed Zibby aside and huddled over the dolls. "'And now with the power invested in me as a minister of God,'" said the butler-minister in the dollhouse hall, "'I now pronounce you man and — whoops!'" Laura-Jane tipped the mother doll over on the floor, then pulled the porcelain head off the little stuffed body with a vicious tug.

Zibby opened her mouth to protest, but Laura-Jane's voice chattered on.

"'Oh, dear me,'" she made the butler-minister say in a hearty voice. "'I'm afraid the bride has fainted. No —

no, I'm wrong, she hasn't fainted — she's died! Massive brain hemorrhage just at the crucial second. But, oh, well, that's the way it goes, folks. Too bad —'"

Zibby shoved Laura-Jane out of the way and grabbed up the dolls. "You are *disgusting!*" she shrieked at Laura-Jane. "I hate you! How dare you!" She raised her hand to slap Laura-Jane as hard as she could, but stopped as she heard Nell's sharp voice from the doorway.

"Zibby! I'm ashamed of you. What in the world are you doing to Laura-Jane? That is no way to treat a guest, and Laura-Jane is not just any guest. Laura-Jane is going to be your *sister.*"

Ned and Brady stepped into the bedroom behind Nell. Ned looked perplexed, his usually merry face creased into a frown. "What's going on here, girls?" he asked.

Zibby was so angry at Laura-Jane she was shaking. Laura-Jane sat there on the rug looking innocent, but her dark eyes challenged Zibby to tattle. Zibby bit her lip. She held up the headless doll for them to see.

Nell reached out and took the doll. "It's all right," she said. "I can reattach the head with a piece of wire and a few stitches. It's nothing to fight about. These dolls are antiques, remember, and fragile. Accidents happen."

"I just wanted to play with the dollhouse," Laura-Jane murmured in a sorrowful baby voice. "But Zibby said I shouldn't touch it."

"That's not what happened and you know it," snapped Zibby.

"Yes it is. You said I shouldn't touch it!" Laura-Jane jumped up and clung to Ned's hand. "Let's go home, Daddy," she whispered urgently. "I don't want to play with her anymore."

"I'll speak to you later, Zibby," Nell said ominously.

Zibby slammed the dollhouse shut and latched it securely. She watched her mom, Ned, Laura-Jane, and Brady walk out of the room and down the hallway. As they started down the stairs, Laura-Jane turned back. She stared at Zibby, then slowly drew a finger across her throat.

# Chapter 3

"At least Miss Honeywell doesn't haunt the doll-house anymore," Jude said soothingly the next morning. "Things could be much worse."

Zibby smiled at her friend. Jude could always be counted on to say something helpful. All the girls had been relieved when Miss Honeywell disappeared and Primrose Parson moved in instead. Primrose had her faults, but she was not dangerous.

The girls were sitting in the shady arbor of their clubhouse in Jude and Penny Jefferson's backyard. Their clubhouse was a spacious room formed when a large tree had toppled in the Jeffersons' backyard during a storm. The higher branches formed a canopy of green for the roof, and other branches made the benches the girls sat upon. It was a peaceful place, perfect for private talks. They hadn't decided where to meet when winter came. For now, the tree was all they needed.

Jude was eleven, the same age as Zibby, and Penny

was a year younger. Jude and Penny looked like sisters, with the same warm brown eyes and dozens of skinny braids in their hair, but they were not sisters at all. The relationship was one that Penny loved to boast about, and one that Jude tried hard to ignore: Penny, though younger, was Jude's *aunt*. Penny's much older brother, Mac, was Jude's father. And since Mac and his wife, Sarah, were doctors working on a special project in a new hospital on the other side of the world, in Kenya, Jude had been sent to live with her grandparents until they returned. And Jude's grandparents, whom she called Noddy and Nana, were also Penny's parents, whom she called — of course — Mom and Dad.

The girls' relationship had been confusing to Zibby when she first met them at the beginning of summer after their move to Carroway from Pennsylvania. But now she hardly thought about it, unless Penny was teasing Jude, or vice versa.

They had formed a club to try to deal with the haunted dollhouse. And they'd solved the mystery of the haunting, but now they still had Primrose Parson to deal with. Charlotte Wheeler, Zibby's cousin, was the fourth member of their club. Even though Charlotte got on Zibby's nerves with her snobby manners and assumed sophistication, Zibby had to admit Charlotte had some good ideas and could be a lot of fun when she wasn't putting on her oh-so-grown-up airs and flipping her blonde mane of hair over her shoulders like some stuck-up fashion model.

Zibby had called a meeting of the club right after breakfast. She needed to tell them about Laura-Jane's unpleasant game with the dolls the night before. "She's horrible," she said. "I can't stand the thought that she's going to be my stepsister."

"Ugh," agreed Charlotte. "And my stepcousin. How did a nice man like Ned get such a jerk for a daughter? And her hair — can you believe it? She looks about six years old with those ponytails and ribbons."

"That's really nasty about the doll," said Penny, making a face. "Did your mom get its head back on yet?"

"Yes," said Zibby. "She reattached it and gave it back to me after breakfast — but not before she gave me a lecture on being nice to Laura-Jane. She was really mad."

"Didn't you tell her what Laura-Jane did?" asked Penny.

Zibby sighed. "I tried — but I didn't want to go into the details of what Laura-Jane played with the dolls."

"Why not?" pressed Penny.

Charlotte raised her brows. "Oh come on, Penny. Poor Aunt Nell is getting married in a couple days. It might freak her out to know she's getting a maniac for a stepdaughter."

"Yeah, but I think she should know."

"I'll tell her next time Laura-Jane does something horrible," said Zibby. "*If* she does." She looked around at the faces of the other girls hopefully. "But maybe she won't. Maybe she's got it all out of her system now."

Jude picked at the bark of the tree branch she was sitting on. "Well, just to be on the safe side, I don't think you should let her play with the dollhouse, Zibby. I mean, *we* know about Primrose and Miss Honeywell, and all of it. But she doesn't. And what if Primrose somehow — I don't know — made herself known? It doesn't sound like Laura-Jane is the sort of girl we'd want to have in on the secret."

Charlotte snorted. "Yeah, we can hardly trust a girl who wants to kill Aunt Nell."

"Well, it was just a game," Penny reminded them.

"Yeah," said Jude, "but a couple months back it wouldn't have been. When Miss Honeywell was still around."

The girls sat quietly for a moment, contemplating the truth in that. Then Zibby brought up something else that was bothering her.

"It's about Primrose. I thought if I locked her in the house, she'd be there — like a prisoner, I guess — when I opened it up again. But when Laura-Jane opened the house, there was no sign of Primrose." Usually Zibby could see signs of the ghost because furniture was rearranged, or the doll had moved. "There was — nothing. And when I picked up the little girl doll, she felt different."

"Different?" asked Jude. "How?"

"Lighter, somehow." Zibby frowned.

"Maybe she's just mad at you," suggested Penny. "She'll get over it."

"I don't know." Zibby tipped back her head and stared up at the leaves overhead. They stirred in the warm summer air. "She's not speaking to me. I haven't heard from her since yesterday." Zibby didn't add how strange it felt after hearing Primrose's piping voice in her head all summer to have this sudden silence. She was surprised that she missed Primrose.

"Oh, she's just sulking," said Penny sagely.

"And you'd be the first to know sulking when you see it," teased Jude.

Penny made a face. "But, really. I can't imagine Primrose being mad for long. Remember how much she wanted to live in the dollhouse! I think she's a nice ghost at heart."

"Ghosts don't have hearts," Charlotte pointed out witheringly. "And I'm not so sure she's nice. I didn't like her much as an old woman, and I don't like her now."

"I think she's gone."

"What?" Jude stared at Zibby.

"I mean it. I don't think she's there anymore."

"Not in there anymore!" cried Penny.

Zibby shrugged. "Just a feeling. The dollhouse seems empty. And the doll was so light."

"But where could she be if not there?" asked Charlotte.

Zibby shook her head. "I don't know. But she's mad at me about those stupid pictures for her walls, and she's gone away. I know I should feel relieved, but it makes me feel creepy. At least when you have a ghost in your dollhouse, you know where she is."

The wind rustled the branches overhead and Penny giggled. "I'll bet that's Primrose now, flying past."

"On her broomstick?" asked Charlotte. "No, that's witches, not ghosts. And there aren't any such things as witches."

"*Or are there?*" teased Jude in a spooky, sepulchral voice, and the girls looked at each other and laughed. Whoever would have thought, when summer first began, that by summer's end they'd all believe, without a shadow of a doubt, in ghosts?

Who could ever be sure what was impossible? Zibby shivered suddenly, feeling the chill of autumn in the summer's air.

After lunch Zibby and Nell drove to Columbus to the shopping mall to pick up the bridesmaids' dresses. They had planned to take Laura-Jane as well, but Ned phoned to say she'd gone out for a bike ride and hadn't come back yet, so they should go on without her. Zibby was relieved because she wasn't looking forward to seeing Laura-Jane again at all.

The bridesmaids' dresses were billowy blue sundresses with big sashes. Nell had ordered them specially, and was pleased because they would be dresses the girls could wear again. On the way to the mall, Nell and Zibby had been talking cheerfully about the upcoming wedding, but on the way home Nell brought up the scene she'd walked in on the night before. It was inexcusable, she said, and Zibby was to apologize to Laura-Jane for her rudeness. "Is that clear?" asked Nell. "I know you might not like the idea of having siblings after being an only child for all your life, but you'll just have to get used to it. Sharing things like your dollhouse is a good way to start."

"Mom, I *don't* mind about having a stepsister and brother. I really don't!" Zibby tried to explain without telling her mom the real reason she'd been so furious at Laura-Jane. No reason to depress her with the news that her beloved soon-to-be stepdaughter secretly hoped she'd die before the wedding. "And I *will* share my things. It's just that — well, Brady is fine. Loud, but fine. I'll get used to him. But Laura-Jane has a mean streak. You haven't noticed it because she's always so quiet, but it's there. I don't like her. And I don't like how she whispers all the time. It's totally creepy."

"I think she's had a hard time with her parents' divorce," Nell said, glancing over at her daughter as she turned the car into the driveway. "Ned told me she started whispering before the divorce — it was almost as if she grew quieter and quieter as Ned and Janet's relationship grew louder and more unhappy. He thinks it's become a habit now. I think she's a very troubled kid — and doesn't have a lot of friends to talk things over with. So just try a little harder, okay?"

Zibby wasn't surprised to hear that Laura-Jane

didn't have many friends. The surprise was that she had any at all. But she nodded. "I'll try," she told her mom.

Ned's van was already parked in the driveway. After this weekend, Zibby supposed, she'd get used to seeing it there all the time. He was spending more and more time at their house, and soon would live there. Today he was getting the attic bedrooms ready for his children. Then, in the evening, they would all of them together be going to Gram and Gramps' house for a celebratory dinner. Charlotte and her family would be there, too. Charlotte's mom, Aunt Linnea, was Nell's sister. Charlotte's dad, Uncle David, had been good friends with Ned back in high school.

Zibby steeled herself as she entered the house, ready to smile and greet Laura-Jane and try to forget about last night, but Laura-Jane was nowhere in sight. Ned came downstairs to greet them. He was wearing old denim overalls spotted liberally with white paint. He looked annoyed.

"Brady is here with me," he said. "But Laura-Jane went off after lunch on her bike and hasn't come back. I left her a note and told her to ride over here as soon as she came in, but she still hasn't come."

"I'm sure she's fine," said Nell soothingly. "But why don't you phone and see if she's there?"

"I have been phoning," he grumbled. "And there's no answer."

"Well," said Nell optimistically. "She might be listening to music with headphones on. . . . Why don't we walk over there now and check if she came in and didn't see your note or something. Fresh air might blow away my headache — I've had it all morning." She stood on tiptoe to kiss his cheek. "Mmmm. My favorite aftershave. *Eau de* White Paint."

He hugged her. "And who said you weren't good at foreign languages?"

Zibby left them kissing in the hallway, and went upstairs to see the attic rooms. They looked much better already, since the junk had been cleared out, the floors had been swept, and now the walls were a fresh, clean white. Brady was standing by the dormer window in his room, looking out. From the back, he looked unusually small. She wasn't used to seeing him so still.

"Hi," Zibby greeted him, and he turned with his ready grin. "It looks nicer up here already, don't you think?" she asked.

"Yeah," he agreed. "It's kind of empty, though. This one is going to be my room. My very own. Dad said. My room at my mom's is bigger than this, but it's kind of messy. And at my dad's apartment, the whole place is a mess, but that's because of Laura-Jane. She has tons of junk. It'll be cool, having my *own* room here."

"Probably this one will be messy, too, once your toys and stuff are all moved up here," Zibby pointed out.

"That's okay. If it's messy with my *own* stuff, it feels like home — wherever I am."

It must be hard, Zibby decided as she looked at him, being only in kindergarten and having to move back and forth between two houses all the time. She was glad that she didn't have to travel to Italy every few months to live with her dad. As much as she hoped to go visit him, she wanted only one place to call home.

Zibby took Brady down for a snack while Nell and Ned went out to look for Laura-Jane. After they'd finished their fruit and cookies, she took him up to her room to dig in the back of her closet for her softball and bat. She was planning to take him out in the backyard and keep him busy until Ned and her mom returned. While she searched in the closet, he started jumping up and down on her bed.

"Hey, don't do that," Zibby said, emerging from her closet with the bat and ball.

"I like to," he said simply, still jumping. "I wanna be like the pizza boy. He has a real trampoline, you know."

Zibby didn't know what he was talking about, and so just walked over and pulled him off the bed. "Come on, let's go outside."

He came along agreeably, still chattering about trampolines. "He let me go on it for a minute, but he let Laura-Jane go on it *longer*. That wasn't fair, was it, Zibby?"

"Mmm," she said, not really listening. Brady tended to chatter so much, she just tuned him out. But since he just kept on chattering, he never really noticed.

She pitched the softball for him to hit until Ned and Nell came walking back from Ned's apartment. They didn't have Laura-Jane with them, and looked worried. "It isn't like her," Ned was saying. "I can't understand where she could be. I hope nothing's happened to her. She knew very well we were coming here to paint, and then going over to your parents' for dinner."

"Maybe you'd better call Janet," Nell suggested. "Laura-Jane might have ridden her bike back to Fennel Grove — if she didn't want to be with us."

Janet was Laura-Jane and Brady's mother. Ned frowned, but headed inside to use the phone. When Zibby, Brady, and Nell joined him, he was just hanging up, shaking his head. "She's not there, and now Janet is worried, too. She's going to call all of Laura-Jane's friends to ask whether they've seen her today."

"I saw her today," said Brady. "We watched cartoons."

"I know you did, son," said Ned, ruffling Brady's hair. "I saw her then, too. But she went out for a bike ride after lunch, and that's the last time I saw her. And that was hours ago." He and Nell started conferring in low tones by the sink. Zibby could see they were scared.

"The pizza boy saw her when we were jumping, Dad," Brady chattered on. "She could jump really high, even higher than me, and he said she was really good. He said she could be an alphabet."

"A what?" asked Zibby.

"An alphabet, you know. One of those circus ladies that flies through the air." Brady climbed up on a kitchen chair by the table and leaped off. "See? I could be an alphabet, too!"

"Acrobat," corrected Zibby. Then she grabbed his shirt as he pelted past her. "Wait a sec, Brady. Who said Laura-Jane could be an acrobat?"

He stopped and looked up at her. "The pizza boy. I already told you."

"And when did he say this?" Zibby pressed.

Nell and Ned had stopped talking and were listening to Brady now.

"When we went to his house to go on the trampoline."

Ned knelt down in front of Brady. "And when was this, Brady? Today?"

He nodded. "I rode there on the back of Laura-Jane's bike. It was really fun, Dad. Hey, will you buy me a trampoline for my birthday?"

"Who is this guy?" Ned asked. "Where does he live, what is his name, how did you meet him, and how did you get home?!" His voice was harsh.

"And why didn't you tell us earlier, Brady?" asked Nell. "You know we're trying to find Laura-Jane!"

"I did tell you!" the little boy cried. "I told Zibby that the pizza boy took us on the trampoline today!"

Zibby shook her head. "I'm sorry, I didn't know what he was talking about."

"I still don't," said Ned. "Okay, Brady, try to make it clear now. We want to find Laura-Jane. Who is this pizza boy?"

"Well, I don't exactly know his name." Brady looked around the kitchen. "Hey, can I have a cookie? I'm getting hungry again."

"Let's clear this up first," said Ned, and Zibby knew he was trying hard to be patient. "Where did Laura-Jane meet this boy?"

"At the restaurant where we had pizza," Brady said readily. He didn't seem to understand what all the fuss was about. "We were playing the video game where the good guys do leaps and somersaults and stuff to knock out the bad guys. And the boy said he could do that kind of stuff, too. And we said, okay, show us — and he said we could come to his house. He has a trampoline, too, and he let us try it! Dad, I want a trampoline, too!"

"Hold on," said Zibby. "You met this guy last night?" She thought back to their dinner in the Italian restaurant. They hadn't met any boy — "Brady, do you mean the waiter? The blond boy who brought our pizzas?"

"Right! He invited us to try out the trampoline. So we went."

Zibby remembered how Brady had been playing the electronic games at the back of the restaurant. And

Laura-Jane had left the table to use the bathroom — also at the back of the restaurant, near the kitchen. She had been gone a long time. Had the boy talked to her then?

Ned had evidently been thinking along the same lines. "Do you remember where his house is, Brady? Can you show me?"

Brady shook his head. "We went fast on Laura-Jane's bike. I don't know which way we went. I just held on tight."

"And how did you get home again?" Nell asked.

"Laura-Jane dropped me off. Then she went back while Daddy was in the shower."

"Enough of this," said Ned abruptly. "I'm phoning the restaurant and asking who their waiter is. Then we'll go over there and see what's happening. This is ridiculous."

"His first name is Todd," remembered Zibby as Ned reached for the phone book. Before he could dial, they all heard the slam of the front screen door. Ned dropped the receiver, and everyone hurried into the front hall.

And there was Laura-Jane. "Sorry I'm late," she said in her soft, sullen voice.

Nell tactfully led Zibby and Brady back to the kitchen and shut the door, but Ned's raised voice could be heard clearly anyway.

"Where in the world have you been?! Have you got any idea how worried we've been? I've been waiting and searching for you, and so has Nell, and so has your mom. Who were you with and why didn't you come home when you were supposed to?"

"I hate you!" rasped Laura-Jane in response. "I was with a friend, that's all, and I was there because I didn't want to be here — with *her* and her stupid daughter! I didn't want to go pick up any stupid bridesmaid's dress, and I don't want to go to any stupid dinner celebration either. Celebrating what? The wrecking of our family!"

Zibby strained to hear Ned's reply, but made out only a low rumbling. She glanced at her mom and saw Nell's cheeks were flushed. Nell busied herself in the kitchen, putting away the clean dishes in the dishwasher, pretending she hadn't heard. Brady, unconcerned, was sitting at the table rolling up balls of paper napkin and resuming his bombing game from the night before.

After another moment, Ned came into the kitchen and took Nell into his arms. "I'm sorry you heard that," he murmured. "You don't deserve it at all."

"Oh, Ned, I had no idea she was so angry," cried Nell, and buried her head on his shoulder. He hugged her hard.

"Don't let her spoil things," he said. "I'll talk to her again. She'll settle down, you'll see."

"I wish —" began Nell. She clutched her head. "I can't think with this raging headache."

"Ssh," he said. "Let's go upstairs and I'll give you a head rub. Or do you need painkillers?" He looked at

Zibby and Brady, still standing there uneasily. "It will work out, kids. But now, we've got a dinner to go to. And I, at least, can't go looking like this." He was still wearing his paint-covered overalls. "Come on, kids. We won't let Laura-Jane spoil things."

Zibby left the kitchen and climbed the stairs to her room, carrying the two bridesmaids' dresses that Nell had left hanging in the hall. *Weddings should be exciting and fun,* she thought with irritation. *With parties and new clothes and flowers, not yelling and crying and insults from mean girls.* Laura-Jane was ruining everything. Even the thought of dinner with Gram and Gramps didn't hold the same promise of fun that it had earlier. Not if Laura-Jane had to be there.

Zibby walked into her bedroom and stopped. She saw Laura-Jane huddled on the floor by the dollhouse. And she saw — no, she only *thought* she saw — a little flash of something gray in one of the little attic windows.

"Well, go ahead," she said sarcastically. "Make yourself right at home. Just try hard not to rip off the heads of any more dolls."

"Sshh," hissed Laura-Jane. "The wedding is about to begin." She had the newly repaired mother and the father dolls in the hall again, with the butler doll standing up as the minister. Zibby forced herself not to rush forward and slam the house shut, right on Laura-Jane's fingers, if that's how it happened. "Dum, dum-de-dum, here we go then, the beautiful bride comes down the aisle. The lovely bridesmaids right in front of her, wearing their gorgeous new dresses — see? Here we are." Laura-Jane indicated two servant dolls propped against the wall.

"So, how was the trampoline?" Zibby asked. "Are you ready to run off to the circus and be an alphabet?" She saw the little girl doll in the blue dress lying on the floor at the side of the dollhouse where she'd left her the night before. The brown braids were flung out to the sides. Zibby picked up the doll. As before, it felt oddly lightweight. How heavy was a spirit, anyway?

Laura-Jane ignored her. Zibby slipped the little doll into her pocket and watched as Laura-Jane marched the groom doll down the aisle to stand by the bride. Then she tipped the minister doll to make him speak. " 'Dearly beloved, we are gathered here today to wit-ness the marriage of these two people, Ned, who al-ready has a wife, but never mind, and Nell-from-Hell, who has come up from the fiery pit to be with us to-day —' "

Zibby clenched her hands into fists, determined to ignore this unpleasant girl who would be her stepsister in only three more days. She hung the bridesmaids' dresses in her closet and pulled her favorite green sun-dress off its hanger. She would wear it to dinner tonight. She would hang out with her cousins Char-lotte and Owen, and with little Brady, and they would have fun. Never mind about Laura-Jane and her mean-spirited play. Resolutely, she carried the green dress with her, heading toward the bathroom to change.

She almost went back when she heard Laura-Jane's sudden, melodramatic gasp — but forced herself not to. She stood just outside her bedroom door, listening.

"'Oh, no, call the doctors quickly,'" cried Laura-Jane. "'Oh, dear — the bride is bleeding from the mouth! Oh, horrors, she's bleeding from the eyes — and now the ears. Oh, wait — it's too late. She's dead and gone. Well, never mind. These things happen from time to time. I'm a minister, after all, and I know about death from all the funeral services I've conducted. You didn't think ministers only do weddings, did you? Take it from me, this is a signal from God to go home to your wife and children. Just leave the bride on the floor, go on. I'll mop up the mess.'"

"Primrose, if you're there, this is your signal to rise up and smash Laura-Jane right in the nose," whispered Zibby fiercely, pulling the little doll with the brown braids and the blue dress from the pocket of her shorts. "Go on! You're a ghost, so *haunt* her already! Scare her out of her skull! She deserves it."

Zibby waited for the answering voice in her head, but it didn't come. And from the sound of Laura-Jane's nasty chuckling in the bedroom, nothing had happened in there, either.

"Primrose?" whispered Zibby again, shaking the doll. "Come on, where are you?"

Nothing.

She sighed, stowing the doll back in her pocket. Then she went into the bathroom, closing the door on Laura-Jane's laughter echoing down the hall. She felt very much alone.

# Chapter 4

Saturday dawned clear and sunny. Zibby woke up in a happy mood, looking out the window at the sunshine. It was a good omen for the wedding. She lay back in bed staring up at the ceiling, listening to the noises of the early-morning house. Birds singing outside her window. Her mom singing along to the radio down in the kitchen. A car *whooshing* past in the street. A scratching from the dollhouse — Zibby sat up abruptly.

Was Primrose back at last? She bounded out of bed and ran to the dollhouse. "Primrose?" whispered Zibby.

No answer. The dollhouse was just as Laura-Jane had left it, with the mother and father dolls lying on the floor in the hall, and the servant and butler dolls propped up against the walls. Zibby snatched them up and laid them gently on various beds in the little bedrooms upstairs.

"Primrose?" Zibby called again, softly. She reached

over for her blue jeans, left in a pile on the floor by her bed, and dug in the pocket. She withdrew the little girl doll with the brown braids, smoothed the blue dress. "Are you back again?" But there was no answering voice in her head. *Primrose must still be sulking*, Zibby decided. She sat thinking about how she might be able to lure Primrose back, then wondered why she wanted to. She decided to talk things over with the other girls when her mom and Ned were away on their honeymoon this weekend.

The newlyweds were not planning a long honeymoon. Their work schedules would not allow for much time away, but they had arranged to splurge on two nights at a luxurious hotel on the shores of Chippewa Lake. Then Ned had to be back in Carroway on Monday to work on the *Gazette*, and Nell had several catering engagements booked for that next week. She was not catering her own wedding, however, gratefully agreeing to leave the details of the reception after the ceremony to Aunt Linnea. Nell and Ned would be leaving for their honeymoon from Aunt Linnea's house after the wedding, and Zibby would stay for the weekend there with Charlotte. Laura-Jane and Brady would be in Fennel Grove with their mother.

*That was a relief*, Zibby thought as she went down to breakfast. The less time she spent with Laura-Jane, the better. She hadn't seen Laura-Jane at all yesterday, and that was the way she liked it. Yesterday Zibby and her mom had spent most of the day together. They'd walked over to Gram and Gramps' house on the other side of town and stayed for lunch, then worked in the garden with Gramps. They'd come home grimy and tired. Zibby's nose was sunburned, but Nell had worn a big hat to escape the sun. "I don't need a red nose to clash with my wedding dress," she'd said.

*Mom looks beautiful this morning*, Zibby thought, *and she isn't even dressed in her wedding finery yet.* Nell sat at the breakfast table with her red-gold hair pulled carelessly back in a shining ponytail, wearing a loose light blue T-shirt and jeans. The newspaper was open on the table in front of her, and she held a mug of coffee, but she was not reading the paper and her mug of coffee had grown cold. She was staring into space with a dreamy smile on her lips.

"Mom, I hate to admit it, but you look like someone in love!" Zibby greeted her.

"Oh, I am, honey." Nell grinned and put down her mug. "Believe me, I am. In fact, I feel I've been waiting for this day all my life. I've been in love with Ned since we were teenagers."

Zibby bit her lip and walked over to the counter to pour herself a bowl of cereal. The mail had arrived and lay on the counter. There was a postcard with familiar Italian stamps from her dad. The picture on the front was of a dark-haired girl picking grapes. Zibby picked it up and read it. As usual it was short, but sweet.

*Dear Zib —*

*Sofia and I thought of you today when we drove to the vineyards for wine-tasting. The girl in the photo is your age, and is the daughter of the vintner. She would like to meet you. I am keeping a list of all the museums and sights we want to show you, and have added "vineyards" to it. We hope you'll visit us here next summer. Let's plan on it. In the meantime take good care. Give my best to your mom and Ned. And a kiss for you.*

*Love,*
*Dad and Sofia*

Zibby carried her cereal and the postcard to the table and sat down. She handed the card to her mom, who read it with a smile. "Vineyards this week, is it? Last week it was Vatican City. Sounds like he and Sofia keep themselves pretty busy. But that's just like your dad. Still playing the tourist even after being there two years. He never did take time just to sit home and relax."

"Did you ever love Dad, Mom?" Zibby asked suddenly. "I mean, you said you always loved *Ned*. So why didn't you marry him in the first place? Why did you marry Dad instead?"

"Oh, honey," said Nell. "I did love your dad. I wouldn't have married him if I hadn't. You see, I'd known Ned for years — he was my school friend, and then my high-school boyfriend. We had never known

50

anyone else, really. I'd never dated anyone else. So when I went off to college and met your dad, he was exciting and different. He was older, and I felt more grown-up when I was with him than I did with Ned. Your dad is very different from Ned, very reasonable and steady. I sometimes used to think he was born all grown-up! He is a good man, reliable and organized and methodical, and always very busy and very, very . . . practical."

"You make Dad sound boring," Zibby protested. She picked up the postcard and smoothed the stamp.

Nell rubbed the back of her neck. Zibby wondered whether her mom's head were aching again. Probably all the stress of having Laura-Jane around, coupled with the wedding preparations were bringing on tension headaches. "No, honey, your dad wasn't exactly boring," Nell said slowly. "He was — predictable. Not really so fun to be with. For me, I mean."

"And Ned makes you laugh," said Zibby.

"Yes," nodded Nell. "He makes me laugh, and he makes me feel that life is full of wonder, with all sorts of unexpected possibilites. And yet he's a quiet, peaceful sort of man. He doesn't have half the energy your dad does. Yet I know we'll be happy together, and I'm lucky that we found each other again when we were both free to come together."

Zibby looked at the postcard, feeling strangely sad and happy mixed together. Sad that her parents hadn't been better suited to each other, but happy that they had each found the sort of person they wanted to live with in the end.

For a moment she thought of Laura-Jane, so angry about her parents' divorce, and so sure that Nell was the evil force dragging them apart. Zibby wondered whether Ned's first wife, Janet, felt the same as Laura-Jane, or whether she wished Ned well. It didn't seem the sort of thing she could talk to Laura-Jane about, though, so Zibby pushed it out of her mind.

She went to phone Jude. Jude and Penny would be at the wedding, along with Mr. and Mrs. Jefferson. The girls were excited, and Zibby talked until it was nearly time to get dressed to go. Gram and Gramps came by to see if they could help with anything. Gramps's truck was full of flowers from his garden, ready to be taken over to the church. Gram stayed behind to help Nell dress for the ceremony, and they arranged to meet again at the church in an hour.

Nell's dress wasn't long and white — white was reserved for first-time brides, Gram told Zibby — but was short and airy, in a beautiful cream color with swirls of shimmery gold thread.

It wasn't hard for Zibby to dress in her blue bridesmaid's dress. She zipped it up and twirled in front of the long mirror in Nell's room, feeling like a princess. Then Gram brushed Zibby's hair until it formed a shining cap, and tucked the hairbrush into the little blue drawstring purse that had come with the dress. When

Gram wasn't looking, Zibby tucked the little Primrose doll in as well, listening for the ghost's voice and hearing nothing. Then Gram set to work on Nell's hair, twisting it up into a soft bun with loose tendrils to frame her face.

They drove to the church, and Aunt Linnea and Uncle David were already there, with Charlotte and Owen in their best clothes. Ned's parents were waiting, too, and his brother James and James's family. There were friends of Ned's and Nell's from their school days, people Zibby didn't know at all from Ned's office, and people she did know who helped Nell with her catering business. In a move designed to disarm the jealousy of the new caterers in town, Nell had even invited Hilda and Hector Ballantyne. Nell pointed them out to Zibby as they marched into the church.

Hilda strutted up the stone steps in a peacock blue dress, her black hair swept high and secured with a blue-feathered comb. Jewels dripped from her ears and neck and sparkled on her fingers. Behind her came Hector, tall and weedy, wearing a creased black suit and shiny black shoes. He sported a thin mustache that he stroked the whole time his wife was speaking. His face wore a look of disdainful amusement.

Hilda Ballantyne greeted Nell effusively and Hector took Nell's hand with a languid bow. "I see you've managed to combine a career with motherhood," Hilda said when Nell introduced her to Zibby. Her voice was deep with a touch of an accent Zibby supposed must be French. Her eyes swept Zibby up and down. "Lovely child. But it must be so difficult for you, my dear. I'm afraid catering, like mothering, requires complete devotion to the art. One can't do either part-time — at least not if one wants to do well." She smiled condescendingly.

Zibby bristled. "My mom does both well! And all her clients love her food!"

"So I hear around town," drawled Hilda. "Your little Patty-cakes has quite a reputation."

"DaisyCakes," Nell corrected her. "And —"

"Whatever," interrupted Hector curtly. "Well, you'll have to work hard to stay in business now that we've arrived, my dear." He laughed shortly, but Zibby knew he didn't mean to make a joke.

Nell smiled briefly, then turned away to greet the other arrivals. There were neighbors from across the street, and then the Jeffersons arrived with Jude and Penny looking resplendent and unfamiliar in their best dresses. Zibby said hello with a big grin.

"Where's the evil stepsister?" asked Jude in a low voice, and Zibby shrugged. But then she popped outside to see whether Ned had arrived yet with Laura-Jane and Brady.

Ned arrived moments later, and he looked very impressive in his suit. Little Brady made everyone smile as he marched up sporting a bow tie, with a flower in his buttonhole.

But where was Laura-Jane?

As much as she had not been looking forward to seeing her almost-stepsister, Zibby wanted to see her now. Laura-Jane wouldn't be out jumping on some boy's trampoline on the morning of her dad's wedding!

Or would she?

Zibby ran over to Ned, the skirt of her blue dress billowing out as she moved. "Where is Laura-Jane? Why didn't she come in with you and Brady?"

Ned smiled at her. "You look lovely, Zibby. That blue suits you. And I'll bet Laura-Jane looks every bit as beautiful — we'll know soon. I'm sure she'll be here any minute."

"She spent last night at her mother's," Nell told Zibby. "But she promised to be here on time, and Janet knows where the church is. So — why don't you and Brady go stand outside the door and watch for their car?"

Zibby and Brady obediently went to stand outside. "It's a red car," Brady said.

Zibby could hear the organ music inside, and knew that the people who had come to the wedding were wondering why they were late getting started. *I'll kill Laura-Jane if she spoils things,* Zibby thought fiercely.

*Just like you'd kill me if you could?* came a voice inside Zibby's head, and she nearly sat down on the steps of the church in surprise.

"Primrose?" Zibby whispered, turning away so Brady wouldn't hear her talking — seemingly to herself. "You've come back!"

*I've come to see the wedding. I love weddings. But I'm not coming back to live with someone as mean as you.*

"But you threatened me, Primrose! You were being greedy and rude, and then *you* started getting mean."

*You said you'd kill me.*

"Well, I'm sorry about that." She scanned the street. "Look, Primrose, Laura-Jane is supposed to be here by now, but she's late. Do you have any idea where she might be?"

*Oh, so now you want my help, do you?*

"Well, yes I do," admitted Zibby.

*Ha!* crowed Primrose. *Miss High-and-Mighty has need of my services after all! Well, I don't know if you deserve them, after the way you've treated me.*

Zibby scowled. She didn't want to fight with Primrose. She just wanted the ghost to understand that she couldn't spend all her time making things for the dollhouse. "How about this, Primrose," she said. "Let's make a deal. You help me out when I need help, and I'll pay you for your — your services — with things for the dollhouse. Framed stamps, if you want. And Charlotte was going to make you a chandelier. Would you like that?"

*I'll think about it,* said Primrose huffily. *It would be a start.* There was a pause while Ned and Nell came outside onto the steps and looked up and down the street. They exchanged a worried glance and went back inside.

*Better late than never,* came Primrose's voice in Zibby's head. *That's a cliché, you know, but you'd be surprised how often clichés are true* — Her little voice disappeared in the clatter of an old black bicycle as it teetered around the corner and pulled up to the curb. Though the rider's helmet obscured most of his blond hair, Zibby recognized him as the waiter from the restaurant — Laura-Jane's pizza boy. And there was Laura-Jane herself, perched on the back fender, her blue dress bundled up around her waist in a froth of delicate cloth.

"Thanks, Todd! See you after!" Her voice didn't sound sullen or whispery at all. It was excited and cheerful, and very young. Hearing it reminded Zibby that Laura-Jane was only ten and a half years old. The same age as Penny. Too young, really, to hang out with a teenage boy.

The boy waved cheerfully and set off again.

Laura-Jane looked at Brady and Zibby standing in front of the church. When she spoke, her voice was back to its usual rasp. "So, all ready for the happy event?"

"You nearly missed it," snapped Zibby. "But that was your plan, wasn't it? To get here late and ruin everything? I'm surprised you showed up at all. Or are you here so you can kill off my mom for real this time?" She glared at Laura-Jane. "Got a knife hidden in your pocket?"

Laura-Jane frowned at her. "These bridesmaids' dresses don't have pockets." She held up her wrist with her blue drawstring purse dangling. "And my bag's too small. Too bad."

Zibby turned on her heel, not trusting herself to say another word, and led the way up the steps into the church. Inside, the organist was still playing. Nell and Ned rushed up when they saw Laura-Jane, their worry and anger plain on their faces. But Gram reached them first and hustled Laura-Jane and Zibby to the door of the sanctuary. She signaled to the organist, who broke off in mid-tune and started playing the wedding processional music that Ned and Nell had chosen. This was the cue for Zibby and Laura-Jane to walk slowly, side by side, down to stand by the altar.

"All right, girls," whispered Gram. "Off you go. Make us proud of you. I'm going to go sit down with Gramps so I can see everything."

Zibby started walking with Laura-Jane. She hoped the other girl wouldn't trip or do anything else to mar the wedding. They passed the Ballantynes who sat near the back, craning their necks as they looked around the church with critical expressions. Zibby smiled as she passed Jude and Penny, sitting with their family, and Charlotte, sitting with Aunt Linnea and Uncle David. Charlotte had applied makeup with a heavy hand. Her cheeks were pink, her lips were red, and her eyes were rimmed in some dark stuff that made her look like a raccoon. Zibby bit back a giggle. Her cousin Owen gave her the thumbs-up sign as she and Laura-Jane glided past in their blue dresses.

Then they were at the altar, and turned to wait for the others. Next came Brady, looking very sweet, with no sign of his usual boisterousness, carrying the ring on a little satin pillow. When he reached the girls, he grinned and stood with them. "I didn't drop it!" he said in a stage whisper.

"Shh!" Zibby said. She glanced at Laura-Jane, and was surprised to see tears glistening on the other girl's cheeks. Then she looked down the aisle, and understood why. Lots of people cried at weddings, but Laura-Jane's tears were not tears of joy.

There came Ned and Nell together, side by side. Ned was so dark with his black hair and dark suit and Nell was so fair with her red-gold hair and silky cream dress, yet they seemed a perfect match. They strolled along, nodding to friends and relatives as if they were walking anywhere, down the beach or along a garden path. They seemed perfectly at ease. When they reached the altar, they faced the minister with smiles.

Zibby had to smile, too. Brady giggled and Laura-Jane poked him, lowering her head and staring at the floor.

The service went off without a hitch. Zibby heaved a big sigh of relief as the minister pronounced Ned and her mom "husband and wife." She walked back down the aisle after the bride and groom with a light step, and joined in the hugs and congratulations on the steps of the church outside. Laura-Jane slipped away and stood by herself. *But at least,* Zibby thought thankfully, *she hadn't done anything to ruin the wedding.* That was a good sign.

Afterward, when they arrived at Aunt Linnea's grandly elegant house for the reception, Laura-Jane barely said a word to anyone, but Brady was everywhere, boisterous and excited. The guests piled gifts wrapped in glittery paper on top of the grand piano in the large living room. Even the Ballantynes had brought a gift, Zibby noted.

She stood talking to Charlotte and Jude and Penny while Ned and Nell cooed to each other in Aunt Linnea's living room and all their friends snapped photos. After the photographs had been taken, Aunt Linnea motioned for the girls to come to the kitchen.

"Would you mind checking that everything is ready in the dining room? I'd like to start bringing people in for lunch in about five minutes."

"No problem," said Charlotte.

Zibby looked around the big dining room with appreciation. The long, antique mahogany table was polished and gleaming. Silver candlesticks held tall cream-colored candles placed at both ends. The centerpiece was the wedding cake — a three-tiered creation covered in luscious swirls of frosting and strewn with real flowers. The top layer was decorated with the traditional figurines of a bride and a groom.

"Ooh," breathed Penny. "It's gorgeous!"

"I think I'd get married just to have a cake like this one!" said Jude.

"Yeah," agreed Zibby. "But I hope Aunt Linnea

didn't order it from the Ballantynes. They're the new caterers in town, and they're really slimy. Their food probably has rats in it."

"Well, we're safe. She ordered it from a bakery in Fennel Grove." Charlotte tossed back her long blonde hair. "Although I must say, *I* think the bride and groom on top are really sort of tacky, but my mom said it's the sort of thing Aunt Nell and Ned — I guess I have to call him Uncle Ned now, don't I? — go for."

"Are you calling my mom *tacky?*" Zibby glared at Charlotte across the table.

"No. I just said my mom said she and Ned like funny things."

Zibby knew it was true that her mom would think the little bride and groom dolls were cute. She thought they were pretty cute herself.

Jude started for the kitchen. "Come on. We're supposed to be bringing in the food."

Laura-Jane stayed in the dining room, sullen and silent, staring into Aunt Linnea's exquisitely furnished dollhouse mansion. The dollhouse, a collector's dream, was on display in one corner. The other girls followed Jude into the kitchen.

The kitchen counters were covered with trays of food. The caterers had prepared all sorts of dips and fresh breads, little sandwiches and quiches, casseroles and salads. There were platters of fresh fruits and vegetables, too, and bowls of steamed rice and rolled sushi. The girls carried the heavy trays carefully to the dining room and arranged them around the center-piece. Laura-Jane had left the room.

When everything was ready, Aunt Linnea asked Charlotte and Penny to summon the wedding guests. Zibby and Jude remained, admiring the wedding feast. Zibby reached forward to straighten out the stack of linen napkins. Then she heard a little noise as if a bead had dropped onto the polished table. She turned and clutched Jude's arm.

"What is it?" Jude asked urgently.

"The cake! Look — the bride!" was all Zibby could get out. Then Jude looked and saw what Zibby had seen.

The bride doll had somehow tipped over and lay on her belly in the thick frosting. But worse than that, the tiny plastic head had broken off at the neck.

The bride doll had been beheaded.

# Chapter 5

Both girls stared in horror, then Zibby scooped the bride doll up and began wiping the poor little headless figure with a napkin. Jude stooped to look under the table for the head. "It must be here somewhere," Jude hissed.

"I don't see how it could have broken off!" cried Zibby. "Not all the way to the floor. It would have gotten stuck in one of the other tiers of the cake —" She broke off and peered closely at the other layers. Sure enough, there it was, a pathetic little face staring up from the center of a marzipan flower. Zibby plucked it up and sucked off the icing.

All day she had been looking for signs that the wedding would go well, and go well it had — till now. But this was an omen of a different sort. Zibby darted an uneasy look toward the dining room doors. "We can't let my mom see this," she told Jude.

"We can fix it," Jude hissed back. "If we work fast."
They could hear the bustle and laughter of people

in the living room moving into the hall, toward the dining room. As lightly as a butterfly hovering on a flower petal, Jude's fingers plucked the little head out of Zibby's sweating hand. The guests came trooping into the room, exclaiming at the wonder of the feast before them. Zibby watched as Jude surreptitiously poked her finger into the side of the lowest tier of cake and scooped up a tiny amount of creamy frosting. This she dabbed on the broken neck of the bride's head. Then, glancing hastily around to see that no one was watching, she stretched up and pressed the head back into place on the bride doll.

Zibby held her breath as they waited to see whether the frosting "glue" would hold. It did. After a moment she and Jude backed away from the table and the guests surged forward, reaching for plates and glasses of champagne. Hector and Hilda Ballantyne looked critically at the array of food and sniffed. But no one seemed to notice that anything had gone wrong. *Most importantly*, Zibby thought, Nell *had not noticed*.

Out of the corner of her eye, Zibby caught a glimpse of a woman in a long, gray skirt leaving the room. She stiffened. Miss Honeywell had worn a skirt like that. Zibby edged to the doorway and peered out into the front hallway. No one was there, but Zibby felt sick inside. She remembered how Laura-Jane had killed off the mother doll by pulling its head off. She remembered her mom's recent headaches.

Jude pressed her friend's arm and whispered to her.

"Don't worry about it, Zib. Those little cake dolls are made of the cheapest plastic. It doesn't mean anything."

"But first Laura-Jane was playing that my mom died during the wedding and now —"

"That was just a mean game," Jude said with confidence. "Laura-Jane didn't mess with the bride doll. She wasn't even in the room just now. It's just a coincidence."

"Unless," began Zibby softly. "Unless it's *not*. I mean, first Primrose got mad and left the dollhouse, saying Miss Honeywell could come back, for all she cared. And then Laura-Jane played with the dolls and pulled the mother doll's head off. And my mom started getting headaches. I couldn't be sure there was any connection. But now — this. What if it isn't just a coincidence?"

"You mean —" began Jude, her eyes wide, "what if Miss Honeywell's ghost *has* come back?"

"Right," breathed Zibby. "She's been waiting for Primrose to leave so she could slip back in. And if she's back, then we've got to watch out. Laura-Jane has set things in motion — and now my mom is in terrible danger!"

Zibby wanted desperately to warn her mom, but getting Nell alone was difficult. Every time Zibby thought she'd managed to find a private moment, wedding guests would rush up to hug Nell or chatter about the wedding or ask her and Ned to smile for the camera. Laura-Jane's pizza boy arrived just before the cutting of the cake, and Laura-Jane's smile was dazzling as she welcomed him. "Who invited him?" Zibby asked her new stepsister, and Laura-Jane scowled at her.

"You've got some of your friends here," she retorted. "I guess I can invite some of mine, too!"

"Sorry, sorry," said Zibby hastily. "I didn't know he was your friend. I mean, you just met him. And he's so old."

"He's my friend," Laura-Jane said firmly. "And he's not so old at all. He's just turned sixteen."

"I wouldn't mind having Todd for my friend," Charlotte whispered to Zibby, tossing back her hair. She checked her makeup in the gold-framed hall mirror. "I think he's adorable."

Zibby looked on while Laura-Jane took Todd over to congratulate Nell and Ned. Charlotte was right — Todd *was* adorable. His blond hair fell over his high forehead, and his face lit with a big smile that made people smile back. But his good looks came even more from the way he moved his body. He was tall and slender, with a lean, lithe strength that showed even in the way he shook hands with Ned and Nell, or carried his plate to the table for food. Zibby decided Todd moved like a leopard.

He sat next to Laura-Jane in the living room, balancing a plate of food on his lap and talking animatedly. Zibby noticed how Laura-Jane only picked at her food while she gazed at Todd with shining eyes. *As if he's her hero or something*, thought Zibby scornfully. But she was glad Todd had come. His smile was a beacon of light cutting through her worries, and his presence meant she didn't have to talk to Laura-Jane.

After another hour of feasting and celebration, Nell climbed the grand staircase in the hallway halfway, then tossed her wedding bouquet over her shoulder to the assembled unmarried girls and women waiting below. Zibby jumped up high, trying to catch it — but Laura-Jane was more agile and reached it first. Everyone clapped and teased her that now she would be the next to get married.

Laura-Jane shook her head, her twin dark ponytails swinging forward to hide her blush.

Then Nell and Ned left for their brief honeymoon. All the guests waved them off, then continued to eat and drink and talk and laugh until evening.

Finally Aunt Linnea's big house was quiet. All the guests had departed. Mr. and Mrs. Jefferson had given permission for Penny and Jude to spend the night with Zibby and Charlotte. Aunt Linnea had invited Laura-Jane and Brady to stay overnight, too, but Laura-Jane wanted to go home. Brady wanted to stay and made a bit of a fuss, but in the end Uncle David had driven both Shimizu children to their mother's house in Fennel Grove and Zibby, especially, was not sorry to see them go. Todd left at the same time, by bike.

Zibby and Charlotte and Penny and Jude all sat up

in Charlotte's designer-decorated room. The other girls' rooms were full of stuffed animals, games, books, and toys — but Charlotte sniffed at such childish possessions and for her birthday had asked to have her room redone. Now it was sleek and clean, with a glassed-fronted bookcase to hold her romance books and to display her collection of fine miniature furniture. There was an antique rolltop desk at which she did her schoolwork on the most up-to-date computer, and a double four-poster bed covered with a jet-black quilt. Her beautifully finished dollhouse stood in one corner on a specially built table. It was set onto a base that allowed the house to swivel. Charlotte's dollhouse, which had once been home to her family of dolls and little horses, now housed the fine furniture that Charlotte had started collecting. She kept the house as a showpiece rather than a plaything. There were no toys in sight, but the dresser top was awash with bottles, jars, and tubes of cosmetics. *Makeup* thought Zibby as she settled herself on her cousin's big bed and hugged a black-and-white checked pillow, *is what Char plays with instead.*

Zibby, as president, had called an emergency club meeting. She hugged the pillow to her chest and brought Charlotte and Penny up to date on how the bride from the wedding cake had lost her head, and how Jude had repaired it with icing. "I'm afraid it's an omen," she told them in a hushed voice. "I'm so scared something will happen to my mom. I've got to warn her."

"But what would you say?" asked practical Jude. "Your mom doesn't know anything about the trouble you've had with that dollhouse in the first place."

"What would I say?" Zibby stared at Charlotte's dollhouse without seeing it. She saw instead the face of Primrose Parson's cruel governess. "I'd say, 'Mom, you're in terrible danger because the ghost of Primrose Parson's governess has come back. And we've already had terrible trouble with Miss Honeywell this summer. She's dangerous. She makes whatever we play with in the dollhouse come true in some horrible, twisted sort of way. And your stupid stepdaughter, dear Laura-Jane, played that your head came off. And so —'" Zibby's eyes filled with tears. "It sounds crazy, doesn't it. My mom would never listen. But we all know it's true — every word!"

Zibby heaved a huge breath. The other girls were nodding.

"It does sound crazy," said Charlotte bluntly. She tossed her long hair back in her characteristic gesture. "Aunt Nell would never believe us."

"Unless we could convince her," Jude added.

"How could we?" asked Zibby hopelessly.

Jude shrugged.

"I know!" said Penny suddenly. "We could let her hear the ghost! Zibby, we could get Primrose talking —

you know, complaining and stuff — and then you take hold of your mom's hand. She'll hear Primrose, and then she'll *have* to believe in ghosts. And once she believes in ghosts —"

"But there's one problem," Charlotte pointed out dourly. "Primrose is gone."

"Well, she did come back for the wedding," Zibby said. "Just for a minute. I asked her to help get Laura-Jane there on time."

"You didn't tell us!" cried Jude. "Did she help?"

"I'm not sure. I mean, I asked her to help get Laura-Jane to the church so the wedding wouldn't start late, and then Laura-Jane arrived. But I don't know if Primrose had anything to do with that. Anyway, one thing is certain — and that's that Primrose is still mad at me."

"We'll have to entice her to come back," Jude said. "Give her what she wants. You know. The stamps and everything."

"I'll make her that chandelier," said Charlotte. "I know it would look so beautiful in the dollhouse dining room."

"I hate to give in to her," said Zibby, though, earlier, she herself had thought of the same plan to lure Primrose back to the dollhouse.

"Remember, we're just *assuming* Miss Honeywell is back because Primrose has gone away in a huff," Jude said thoughtfully. "But remember, when Miss Honeywell was here before, you heard bells."

Zibby nodded. That was true. She had heard the peal of the schoolbell the governess had rung to call Primrose to her lessons. And sometimes Zibby had felt a stinging across her palms — the ghostly imprint of Miss Honeywell's ruler, smacking across Primrose's hands.

But this time she had heard no bells, felt no sting.

"So maybe Miss Honeywell isn't there at all," said Jude encouragingly. "Maybe the house is empty."

"After all, nothing has happened to Aunt Nell yet," Charlotte pointed out.

"Except the headaches," Jude said. "But Laura-Jane first played with the dolls — when? Three days ago? I'd think if Miss Honeywell were back, she'd be making bad things happen already. Think how quickly she made things go wrong before."

Penny brightened. "So maybe your mom's not in danger after all, Zibby!"

Zibby tried to smile at the girls' attempts to cheer her up, but in her heart she felt sure something was wrong.

"Well, look," said Charlotte. "Why don't you ask my mom if you can phone their hotel and talk to your mom for a minute. You can just tell her you want her to be extra careful while she's away. You don't have to say anything about ghosts or dollhouses or anything."

Zibby jumped up. "That's a great idea, Char. Thanks!" And she ran downstairs to ask Aunt Linnea for the number. If she could get her mom to take special care to watch out for danger, maybe things would be all right.

Aunt Linnea frowned when Zibby asked to phone her mom, and said that people shouldn't really bother other people who had just gone away on their honeymoon. But Zibby pressed, and Aunt Linnea finally gave her the phone number of the hotel. Zibby jabbed the buttons eagerly and listened to the ringing on the other end. When the receptionist answered, Zibby asked for Nell Thorne and was told there was no one at the hotel by that name. Then Zibby remembered, and asked for Nell *Shimizu*. The receptionist said that Mr. and Mrs. Shimizu had not yet arrived. It made Zibby feel funny to hear her mom referred to as Mrs. Shimizu, but it made her feel even weirder that they hadn't arrived at the hotel. Nell and Ned had left several hours ago, and the lake was only about a forty-minute drive from Carroway. *Of course they might have stopped for dinner along the way,* she told herself. "Well, please ask them to call Zibby when they get in," she told the receptionist. "That's short for Isabel." And the receptionist promised to give them the message.

Zibby tried hard to put the worry out of her head for the rest of the evening and let herself be soothed by her friends. Charlotte offered to make up their faces and give them new hairstyles, but the other girls said that sounded boring. Miffed, Charlotte started sulking, until Jude suggested they all get busy making things for Zibby's dollhouse to entice Primrose to return. So Charlotte took them down to her mother's basement workshop, and they set to work.

Zibby's Aunt Linnea was an avid miniature enthusiast, and collected exquisite furnishings for her own dollhouse, which was a replica of an English stately home. Her dollhouse was not something to be played with, and stood magnificently at one end of the dining room. In her workroom, Aunt Linnea built shadow boxes and decorated miniature rooms to sell at miniature shows. She and Charlotte sometimes worked together designing miniature scenes. Although Charlotte had decided she was too old to play with dolls, she still enjoyed making tiny things to furnish her dollhouse — or Zibby's.

After Charlotte, Penny was the other dollhouse enthusiast in their group. Penny had asked for a dollhouse for her birthday. She was already saving her allowance to buy things for it. Jude and Zibby, who were both good at carpentry, had decided that if Penny didn't get the dollhouse for her birthday, they would build her one together. Neither of them had been especially interested in dolls or dollhouses until the ghost took up residence in Zibby's antique dollhouse. Now they settled down to making things for Primrose just as eagerly as Charlotte and Penny.

Penny decided to make Primrose some more framed paintings, and started cutting pictures out of an old museum catalog Charlotte's mother had tossed into the recycling basket. Charlotte started stitching a tiny pillow from a scrap of flowered fabric stuffed with cotton balls. And Zibby and Jude decided to build a swing for the dollhouse porch.

Aunt Linnea's workshop smelled of wood chips and paint. The big worktable was covered with different shoe boxes and plastic bins full of various materials for making miniature furnishings — balsa wood in different lengths and thicknesses, bottles of woodstain and varnish, paintbrushes and markers and tiny pots of paint, pieces of fabric and ribbon. There was a sewing machine at one end of the table, and a well-equipped toolbox at the other end.

As Zibby cut balsa wood for the little porch swing, she kept wondering whether her mom had arrived at the hotel. She wondered where Primrose was, and what it was like to be a ghost, anyway. She was wondering these things when she heard the phone ring upstairs in the kitchen. She put down her little saw and listened, heart pounding. After a moment Aunt Linnea's voice called down the basement stairs, "Zibby, telephone!"

Zibby raced up the stairs and took the receiver from her aunt. "Mom? Oh, good! I was getting worried. How come you're so late?"

Nell's voice sounded tired. "Oh, Zibby. We had a terrible time getting here. We'd only driven about halfway, when we got a flat tire. And when we stopped to get it fixed, we found out it wasn't just one tire, but all four! We had to walk to a phone and then wait ages for a tow truck. The man at the garage patched them up for us, but it took forever until we were ready to drive on, and so we only just got here."

"I was worrying about you," Zibby said. Then she thought of something. "How come *all four* tires were flat? That's pretty strange."

Nell was silent on the other end of the line. In the silence, Zibby could hear her own heart beating. Then Nell's voice came slowly. "It *is* strange. The man at the garage told us that all four tires had been deliberately punctured."

"Deliberately? What a rotten trick!" Zibby closed her eyes. She'd been right to be so worried.

"It's not the sort of thing any of the wedding guests would have done as a joke," Nell was saying, "so I can't imagine who did it. But anyway, we're here now, and we're starving. Ned's waiting to take me to dinner, but first he wants to say hello to Brady and Laura-Jane."

"Oh, they're not here," said Zibby. "Uncle David took them to Fennel Grove. But Jude and Penny are still here, and we're making dollhouse stuff."

"I hope you made Laura-Jane feel she was welcome," Nell said.

"She didn't *want* to stay," Zibby said defensively. "Anyway, Mom, listen. Don't let anything else happen. Watch out."

"Watch out?" asked Nell with a tired laugh. "For what?"

75

"Oh, I don't know. Watch out for anyone else with rotten tricks in mind, I guess."

"All right," Nell promised. "I'll keep a close eye out!"

She asked one more question. "Mom, how's your head?"

Nell sighed wearily. "Oh, Zibby. It's throbbing worse than ever. I don't think I've ever had such a bad headache. What a bad start to the honeymoon!"

There was nothing Zibby could say to that, but her heart hardened. Miss Honeywell had to be stopped.

# Chapter 6

Three days later Zibby sat on the floor in front of her dollhouse and attached the balsa wood swing to the front porch. Jude had painted it a bright cherry red and attached a little gold chain to each corner. Zibby was now hanging these from the two small hooks she had screwed into the ceiling of the porch.

"Primrose?" she whispered. "Come back and try out your new swing."

No answer. But Zibby wasn't really expecting an answer. It had been almost a week now since her fight with the ghost, and except for that brief appearance just before the wedding, there had been no sign of Primrose. Nor had there been any sign of Miss Honeywell since the report about the four punctured tires. The dollhouse seemed unusually bare, though its eight rooms and attic were full of furniture. Zibby wasn't sure *how*, but she thought she would know if Miss Honeywell was in residence.

Zibby sat back and inspected her swing. It looked

just right. She left the front of the dollhouse unlatched in case Primrose returned, though she thought if ghosts could go through walls, an open dollhouse would be unnecessary. Still, she wanted the house to look welcoming.

She went downstairs. Her mom was in the kitchen making puffs of pastry to fill with olives and cheese. She would be catering a wedding anniversary party the next day. She looked up with a smile when Zibby came in.

Zibby watched her mom chop olives and onions together on a chopping board, wielding the knife so professionally that the food was reduced to a pile of fine slivers in seconds. Nell dumped the pile into a small bowl, and handed Zibby the cheese grater and a large wedge of cheese. "Want to help?"

"Okay," said Zibby, and started grating the hard chunk into the bowl while Nell went to one of the two large refrigerators and started rummaging around. Zibby looked up in alarm as she heard a door close in another room, then relaxed again after a second. "I forgot about Ned," she admitted to Nell, who came back to the table carrying a big mound of chilled pastry dough. "It's kind of hard getting used to having another person in the house again."

"I know," said Nell. "But soon it will seem as if we've always been together. Ned's upstairs now, getting Laura-Jane's and Brady's rooms ready. Soon even Laura-Jane and Brady will feel like family."

Zibby doubted that, but said nothing.

"They'll be arriving this afternoon," Nell reminded her. "And they'll be here until school starts. I'm counting on you to be friendly and make them feel welcome."

Zibby looked up. "I will if they will," she said. Nell frowned at her. Zibby grated the last of the cheese into the bowl. There was one little piece left in her hand, and she popped it into her mouth. "I mean, of course I'll be friendly," she said through her mouthful of cheese. "But Laura-Jane had better be friendly, too."

"Give her time to get used to us," Nell said. "We all have some adjustments to make."

Zibby sat watching while Nell rolled out the pastry dough with deft strokes. She loved watching her mom work. Nell was well-respected as the best caterer in Carroway, whether the Ballantynes liked it or not. She'd begun DaisyCakes as a baked goods service, then expanded her company to full catering after the divorce. It was work Nell loved, but hard work all the same, and Zibby was well aware that the elegant platters of food that looked deceptively simple to make actually demanded a great deal of Nell's time and attention.

Just as Zibby and Nell finished arranging the mounds of food on the trays, Ned called to them from upstairs to ask for help moving some furniture into the new bedrooms for Laura-Jane and Brady. Nell washed her hands quickly, dried them on a tea towel, and hurried from the room. Zibby snatched two tiny quiches from one of the platters and followed more slowly. They tasted buttery and crisp, with a hint of onion, and practically melted in her mouth as she climbed the stairs.

Nell and Ned were easing a long, low bookcase into Laura-Jane's room. Zibby peered around as they set it under the eaves. The attic room looked welcoming. The walls were white and the curtains were made of deep blue gauze. Ned had set up Laura-Jane's oak bed near the door. There was a dresser in one gable and a desk in the other. The cushion on the desk chair, Zibby noted, was one that Gram had needlepointed — a yellow sun and moon and star on a dark blue background. Zibby had always liked that cushion. It used to be downstairs on the chair by the telephone. *Laura-Jane better appreciate it!* she thought.

Nell smiled with satisfaction. "It'll look even nicer once we get her a new quilt for the bed," she told Ned. "Maybe dark blue with stars — like the cushion. If we can find one. I was thinking I'd take Laura-Jane and Brady shopping this weekend and let them choose what they like for their rooms. If I pick it out, I'm bound to be wrong." She reached up and massaged the back of her neck as if it were hurting her again.

Ned looped an arm around her shoulders and hugged her. When they started kissing, Zibby looked away, blushing. She moved out into the narrow hall toward Brady's room to see what had been done in there, but stopped when she heard a series of muffled thuds and bangs from downstairs. She started running down the stairs.

"Wait," hissed Ned, close behind her as Zibby rounded the second flight of stairs. "Let me go first. You never know —" And she waited while he pushed past her. Nell grabbed her hand in alarm.

They stood in the front hallway, listening. But there was only silence. Ned checked the living room. "Nothing," he said.

"What could it have been?" wondered Nell, peering into the small dining room and again finding nothing to explain the crashing sounds.

Zibby went ahead into the kitchen — and stopped. There was no need to look further.

Every single platter of carefully prepared and elegantly presented food now lay scattered on the kitchen floor. The china serving trays were shattered into a thousand pieces. And as if that weren't bad enough, the food had been stomped on, and ground into the kitchen floor. Chocolate smudges led a trail across the room to the back door.

Zibby gasped in horror, and tried to back out of the room, pulling the door closed on the carnage — as if by shutting it out she could somehow keep her mom from seeing it. But Nell and Ned were right behind her in the doorway, and they pushed into the room.

Nell let out a scream, then raised both hands to clutch at her head as if in agony. Ned wrapped his arms around her tightly from behind. "Who could have done this?" Nell cried. "Who? Why?"

Zibby saw a flicker of gray outside the kitchen window, and her stomach churned. She felt she might be sick. She thought she knew, all too well, *who*. And *why?* Did an evil ghost like Miss Honeywell need a reason?

Zibby pressed her hand to her mouth as she regarded the wreckage of all Nell's hard work. The knives, long and sharp, lay amidst the spoiled food. Zibby couldn't bear to think about what would have happened to Nell if she had been in the kitchen when Miss Honeywell appeared, bent on destruction.

"Primrose!" she whispered inwardly. "Where are you when I need you?"

Still no answer.

Nell walked, dazed, into the living room and sank onto the couch. Ned went straight to the phone and called the police. He explained what had happened, then went over to Nell, hovering over her, murmuring words of comfort. Zibby's heart was pounding as she ran upstairs to her bedroom and crouched in front of the dollhouse. Was it her imagination — or was the air charged with something strange? Was Miss Honeywell back, laughing over her cruel attack on Nell? Zibby peered into each of the dollhouse rooms, searching for any sign of the governess. The Primrose doll still lay on the tiny bed where Zibby had left her.

"Primrose?" she called softly. "Come on, come home now. I don't want Miss Honeywell back. I want you instead. Please! My mom is in danger!"

There was no answering voice in her head, but the

little porch swing began swinging ever so gently back and forth. *Had she bumped it?* Zibby wondered. "Primrose, is that you?" No answer.

Zibby heard a car pull up and ran to the window. A red sports car had stopped in front of the house, and Laura-Jane and Brady were climbing out. A hand waved out the window as the two children started for the house, and then the car roared off.

Zibby went back downstairs just as Brady and Laura-Jane came into the front hall. Nell's sobs led them straight into the living room, where they found Ned, still trying to comfort Nell. It frightened Zibby to see her mom so upset. Nell was the sort of person who never cried.

"What is it, Daddy?" asked Brady, running over to them. "What's wrong, Nell?"

Laura-Jane entered more slowly. Zibby was shocked to see a little smile on her stepsister's face. Before Zibby could say anything, Ned explained.

"There's been an attack," he said. "Thank goodness no one was in the kitchen at the time."

"But we were in the h-house," wept Nell, looking up and pushing her hair out of her eyes. "Oh, Ned, what if they'd come looking for us?"

"Who?" asked Brady. "Who was attacked?"

"No one, thankfully," said Ned. "But — well, come and see for yourselves. But don't touch anything. We've called the police and I want them to see it all just the way we found it."

"The *police?*" squealed Laura-Jane. "Why did you do that if no one was hurt?"

Brady ran off toward the kitchen with Ned, Zibby, and Laura-Jane following. Nell remained in the living room, covering her face with her hands as if she couldn't bear to see the destruction of her beautiful work again.

"The police," Ned repeated firmly. "Because someone came into the house while we were upstairs and completely trashed the kitchen. All Nell's work — ruined. For what? By whom? That's what the police need to find out. Destruction of property is a crime. So is trespass."

Laura-Jane, Zibby was glad to see, looked appropriately horrified at the sight of the kitchen. "What a mess," she said in her whispery voice after a moment of silence.

"What will the people whose party Mom was catering do now?" Zibby wondered aloud. "Poor Mom — I don't see how she'll be able to fix things in time for the party tonight."

"She can if we all help," said Ned. "She's worked too hard making this catering business as successful as it is to lose important customers because of someone's viciousness. I'll ask her to write me out a shopping list and after the police see this, I'll go buy the ingredients. You girls can stay here and clean up. Then we'll start cooking."

Zibby and Laura-Jane looked at the mess, then at

each other. "It'll take *hours*," objected Laura-Jane. "And I had *plans*. I was — going to see a friend."

Zibby didn't like the idea of spending the rest of the afternoon cleaning and cooking either, but Laura-Jane's reluctance angered her. "I'm going to see if *my* friends can come over to help us," she announced self-righteously. Jude and Penny would come, she knew, and even Charlotte, who despised anything resembling housework, would come if the work were part of a club effort. "I'm going to phone them now."

"Great idea," Ned said approvingly. "Laura-Jane, why not ask your friend to come by as well? You could make a party of it."

"I want to help, too!" cried Brady. "I'm a good cook!"

"Too many cooks spoil the broth," Laura-Jane said sulkily. "I'm busy today."

"Many hands make light work," retorted her father. "That's the proverb that tells the other side. Now why not go up and see the new bedrooms. After the police leave, we'll start working."

Laura-Jane shook her head obstinately, dark hair swinging. "Dad —"

"Enough!" he snapped. "Your stepmother is very upset, and we all need to help out now. When there's trouble, families pull together."

"She's not my family!" yelled Laura-Jane. Then she bolted out of the kitchen. They could hear her feet pounding up the stairs.

Ned hesitated as if he weren't sure whether to go

after her or not. The arrival of the police made up his mind for him. He went to the door to let them in.

Two police officers, a man and a woman, entered the kitchen. They introduced themselves as Officers Marec and Grayling. The man, Officer Marec, whistled softly at the mess. Officer Grayling whipped a small notepad out of her uniform pocket and started writing down a description of the crime. Ned described what had happened, how they had been upstairs when they'd heard the crashing sounds. How they'd come down to find the destruction. How they had seen no sign of the intruder.

"He must have come in and out the back door," said Ned. "I'm afraid it was unlocked. Probably that's where we went wrong, I don't know —"

"People in Carroway never lock their doors," Zibby said. "At least not in the daytime."

"And it's a shame if it can't remain that sort of small town," said the policewoman grimly.

The policeman nodded. "Too bad the footprints aren't clearer. But we'll dust for fingerprints. See if we can't track down this guy."

Zibby and Brady watched with interest as the police officers dusted the table and countertops and pieces of china and cutlery for fingerprints. "We'll need to take your prints," the policewoman said to Ned. "And the prints of everyone who lives here — just for purposes of elimination."

"Of course." Ned nodded.

"What does that mean, Dad?" asked Brady. He was watching the police with excitement, hopping up and down.

Ned explained that the police needed to check the fingerprints of the people who normally used the kitchen. Then if they found a print that didn't match any of those, they could investigate whose it was.

"Cool!" cried Brady, his dark eyes shining. "Guess what, Dad? Guess what, Zibby? I'm going to be a policeman when I grow up."

Zibby watched silently until the police were done. It was on the tip of her tongue to tell them they didn't need to waste their time. They weren't going to find the prints of any criminal. Ghosts don't leave fingerprints. But she said nothing. When the police officers had spoken to Nell and checked the rest of the house, they drove away in their squad car. Brady started zooming around the house, pretending to drive a police car. Zibby went to phone Jude, Penny, and Charlotte.

She told them briefly what had happened, and they agreed to meet at Zibby's house fifteen minutes later. Zibby waited in the living room with her mom. Nell took some pain relievers for her pounding headache — "Not that it does me any good, these days," she murmured — and pulled herself together to write out a list of things for Ned to buy at the market. He was adamant that if they worked fast, Nell could still be ready to cater the evening party. Never one to be down for long, Nell was entering into the spirit of the race.

"I suppose I could omit the yeasty rolls and make quick bread," she mused. "And I'll make pasta salad with ready-made pasta instead of homemade, since what's on the floor was my last batch." She wrote a few more items on the list. "And we'll have to forget the baklava. Too many layers. I'll make a cake instead. And the tarts will be easy enough, if you can get some good, ripe peaches."

"Will do," said Ned.

Nell pushed back her hair and the half-smile she gave Ned was almost back to normal. "You're a wonder, Ned Shimizu. Giving up a day of work to help me! Now I know why I married you."

"You mean — not for my rugged good looks?" he teased, grinning back at her.

Zibby left the room when they started kissing. But she knew that her own dad would have reacted in a very different way. Of course he would have been sorry Nell's work had been ruined, but he would have left her to clean it up and fix things as best she could, while he returned to work. He wouldn't have been home from work in the first place. In which case Nell might have been in the kitchen when the ghost had arrived . . .

Zibby tried to push back the memory of all the other injuries and disasters that had happened when Miss Honeywell wielded power. She knew her mom had had a very narrow escape that day.

# Chapter 7

Jude and Penny arrived and set to work willingly under Nell's direction. Aunt Linnea drove Charlotte over and stayed to help. Zibby ran upstairs to tell Laura-Jane to come down, but her stepsister's new bedroom door was locked, and Laura-Jane's sullen voice snapped at her through the door. "Go away, I'm busy."

Ned had already left for the grocery store, so Zibby could not tell him about Laura-Jane's refusal to help. But she would, she decided, as soon as he returned.

The hard thing was knowing where to start. The chaos in the kitchen looked impenetrable to Zibby, but Nell and Aunt Linnea took charge and soon made a dent in the mess. First they swept all the food into one gloopy mass and scooped it into a cardboard box to take out to the trash bins. Then Jude and Zibby swept up all the broken glass and china into a large pile by the back door, and Aunt Linnea collected it into a trash bag. Charlotte washed the silver platters and

89

dried them. Penny loaded the unbroken dishes into the dishwasher. Aunt Linnea gave Brady a rag to help wipe up the food on the counters and table. Then Nell washed the floor.

Just as they were finishing, Ned returned with the bags of groceries. "Where's Laura-Jane?" he asked.

"Still upstairs," said Nell. "But please don't drag her down to help. We need only willing workers right now."

Ned scowled, but nodded. And then the cooking began in earnest. All the helpers donned the black cotton cooks' aprons printed with the large yellow daisy that was the DaisyCakes logo. They set to work under Nell's competent direction, and soon pies, cakes, quiches, pasta salads, little delicacies on sticks, plump morsels of cheese and meat paté materialized as if by magic.

"You're all hired!" Nell exclaimed gaily as the assembled helpers put finishing touches on the platters of food. Zibby was arranging sprigs of fresh coriander around slices of focaccia topped with caramelized pear and Brie cheese. She looked up with a smile.

"It's fun. And I think you'll actually get to the job on time."

Nell glanced at the clock. "Yikes! I'd better get changed. Ned, darling, will you start loading the platters into the van?"

He nodded agreeably, but then his face darkened with anger as they heard the screen door in the front hall slam. Zibby ran with him into the hall, just in time to see Laura-Jane speeding down the street on her bike. Ned was furious, but said nothing. He went back to the kitchen and picked up some platters. Zibby half-dreaded, half-looked forward to the scene that would surely erupt when Laura-Jane arrived home. She'd probably be grounded for a year.

*Serves her right*, thought Zibby.

Charlotte and Penny agreed to stay and finish washing up the dishes with Aunt Linnea, but Zibby and Jude decided to ride along to help set up the food. The party was being held at a church hall in the town center for Mr. and Mrs. Gminski, who were celebrating their golden wedding anniversary. "Golden means their fiftieth," whispered Jude after they'd been introduced to the couple. "Can you imagine being married to anybody that long?"

"I can't imagine being that *old*," Zibby replied. "But it's nice that their marriage has lasted. So many people are divorced these days." She glanced at her mom and Ned as they opened the back of the van and started unloading the heavy platters into the hired hall. It would be nice to think they'd found the right match at last, a match that would endure for fifty years.

"We'd wondered if you were coming," said old Mr. Gminski in a querulous voice to Nell. "Thought maybe you'd forgotten."

"No, not at all, Mr. Gminski. I'm afraid we just had

a bit of a muddle — but everything's fine now." Nell's voice was her professional one, smooth and bright. "Of course we couldn't forget an occasion like this!"

The Gminskis' daughter, who was hosting the party, ran up with a flurry of questions and instructions for Nell, and Nell was pulled off to inspect the kitchen facilities. Ned and the girls returned to the van for more of the food platters.

"Hi there," said a friendly voice behind her as Zibby had her head inside the van. She turned, arms laden, to find Laura-Jane's "pizza boy" smiling at her. "I'm Todd, remember? Todd Parkfield."

"I remember you," Zibby said. "Is Laura-Jane with you?"

"No!" He sounded genuinely surprised. "I haven't seen her since — since the wedding, I guess. Why?"

"Oh, just because she ran out when she was sup-posed to be helping —" Zibby broke off. He was cute up close, nicer than she'd remembered. His blond hair had been trimmed and no longer covered his eyes.

"Helping with what?" he asked with a dazzling grin. She had to smile back as he reached for the plat-ter she was carrying. "Here, let *me* help." He tried to peer through the plastic cover. "What is it, anyway?"

"Stuff for a party my mom's catering. You've got the pear and Brie tartlets. That's what Laura-Jane was sup-posed to be helping with." It was on the tip of her tongue to tell him about the attack on the food, but she decided that was information her mom might want to keep quiet about. She pulled out the last platter and led the way into the church hall.

"It smells awesome," Todd said, following behind her.

He stayed to help them set the food out on the buffet table, carefully following Nell's directions. Zibby and Ned worked together, arranging the plates and cutlery. Nell warmed up the heated offerings in the large church kitchen. Jude had a deft hand at flower arranging.

"Beautiful," Nell declared in relief when they were finished. She looked around with satisfaction, then withdrew a box of matches from her black apron. "Let me just light the candles — and we're ready." She flicked the match and held it out to the tall tapers. "There! Perfect — bring on the guests!" She took Ned's arm and gave it a squeeze. "I couldn't have done it without your help. *All* of you. Thanks very much."

Then it was time for Ned and the girls to leave. "Where's Todd Parkfield?" asked Nell. "I want to thank him especially." She looked around. Instead of Todd, she saw Hilda and Hector Ballantyne sauntering around the side of the building. They stopped.

"Catering a little affair this evening, I assume?" purred Hector in his oily voice. He stroked his little mustache.

"It's a rather large affair, actually," Nell said. "But I've been lucky enough to have helpers." She took Ned's arm, and smiled at the girls and Todd, as he emerged from the hall with a shy grin.

"I enjoyed it," he told them. "What are friends for?"

*He'll probably be a good friend for Laura-Jane after all,* thought Zibby. *The big brother she never had. And maybe some of his sweet temper will rub off on her.*

The Ballantynes wished Nell good luck with her party in an overly hearty, completely insincere manner, then strolled slowly down the street.

"Charming people you meet in your business," Ned teased as Zibby and Jude climbed back into the van. Nell rolled her eyes. She seemed in good humor once again, and ready to put the stress of the afternoon behind her.

Ned offered Todd a ride home, but Todd said he'd left his bike parked at the side of the church. So they all said good-bye and left for home. When Zibby looked back, she saw the Ballantynes had stopped strolling down the street and had returned to stand outside the hall. She saw the Ballantynes step closer to the building and peer in through the glass doors. And she thought she also saw, as Ned's van turned the corner, a flash of gray cloth on the other side of the glass.

# Chapter 8

When they drove into the driveway, Laura-Jane's bike was nowhere to be seen. Wherever she'd gone off to, she hadn't decided to return yet. Ned slammed the van into gear, cut the engine, and opened the door. He strode into the house without a word.

*Uh-oh*, thought Zibby, *Laura-Jane's in big trouble.*

"I think I'll just head home now," said Jude brightly.

"Lucky you," muttered Zibby.

"Maybe you could come with me," suggested Jude.

"Thanks, but I guess I'd better stay. Family duty, you know." Was Laura-Jane family now? Zibby didn't know.

Inside she found Ned in the kitchen with Aunt Linnea. Penny had gone home, and Charlotte and Brady were sitting at the table flicking tiny paper balls around.

"Bombs?" inquired Zibby.

"Soccer, you dimwit," returned Charlotte. She flicked the paper wad at Brady and he caught it.

Ned and Aunt Linnea were in consultation by the back door. "Where can she be?" asked Aunt Linnea.

"I don't know." His voice was grim. "Time to make some phone calls."

He had called some of Laura-Jane's friends and Laura-Jane's mother, Janet. No one knew where Laura-Jane was. He was just planning to call the Carroway police when they heard the clatter of Laura-Jane's bike as she leaned it up against the porch.

Ned raced to the door and met Laura-Jane as she was coming up the steps. Zibby hovered in the hallway with Brady and Charlotte. What would Ned do?

He put his hand on Laura-Jane's shoulder and steered her into the kitchen without a word. Aunt Linnea slipped out just as he closed the door.

"I think we'll take ourselves off now, Charlotte my girl," she said lightly. "We'll leave Ned to sort out his daughter on his own."

Zibby and Brady looked at each other. "Uh-oh," said Brady. "Poor Laura-Jane." Zibby marveled that he seemed genuinely sorry that his sister was in trouble. But maybe she didn't act so nasty to little Brady.

Zibby and Brady said good-bye to Aunt Linnea and Charlotte. Then they listened at the kitchen door, but there was no shouting. Only the low rumble of Ned's voice. For a long time.

After what seemed like ages, Laura-Jane, her face streaked with tears, sidled out of the kitchen carrying a sandwich in one hand, and stomped upstairs to her attic bedroom. Zibby was more glad than ever that she and her stepsister didn't have to share a room. After a while Ned walked calmly back into the living room. He was carrying a plate of ham and cheese sandwiches and two apples. "Here you go, kids," he said, sounding weary. "This is supper."

Zibby and Brady each accepted an apple and a sandwich. "What happened to Laura-Jane?" Brady piped up.

"She's grounded for a week," his father said. "That means no bike rides, no playing outside at all — except in the yard. No going anywhere — unless Nell or I take her."

"Where was she?" asked Zibby.

"She says she was just out riding around. But I'm not having kids refuse to help when help is needed, and I'm not having kids jump ship without telling a grown-up where they're going. This behavior is not like Laura-Jane, and it's got to stop."

Ned settled himself into the armchair in the living room with his sandwich and picked up the sports pages. Zibby and Brady ate their supper while they watched a nature program about spiders on TV. Then Ned took Brady upstairs for his bath and story before bedtime.

Zibby had worried that having Ned around the house would be awkward. She had become used to sharing the space only with her mom. When Ned returned and sank comfortably back into the armchair by the window, she continued watching TV for a bit, then wandered upstairs to her room. The dollhouse was open as she'd left it, but one thing was different.

The mother doll had been stuffed into the chimney, headfirst.

Zibby gasped, and ran to rescue the doll, whose tiny legs protruded pathetically from the small opening in the bricks. She peered into the dollhouse rooms for other signs that Miss Honeywell was in residence.

But there was nothing.

Zibby started sweating. The heat from the day seemed to have gathered into the walls of her room. Zibby felt waves of heat pressing out from all sides. She couldn't bear to be in the same room with the dollhouse. She grabbed her pen and box of stationery from her desk, then backed out into the hallway. As she pelted downstairs, she thought of her mom. Did the doll-in-the-chimney mean something else was going to happen to Nell?

She ran back to the living room and sat down on the couch across from Ned. "Can we phone Mom?" she asked urgently.

"She's working, honey," he said absently.

"I know, I know — but —" Zibby stopped. Ned looked up quizzically.

"What's up?" he asked.

"I'm — worried about her. After what happened to the kitchen. I'm afraid something else is going to happen."

Ned nodded. "Understandable. But I'm sure she's fine. The intruder was probably just out to make trouble. I don't think it could have been aimed especially at Nell." He smiled reassuringly. "I'm going to pick her and all her catering equipment up again at eleven o'clock."

"Well, okay," said Zibby slowly. She supposed that if Ned were bringing her mom home, nothing could happen *then*. But what about right now? What if Miss Honeywell's malicious tricks were happening *now*? "But maybe I could call her just to see if she's all right?"

"I really think she wouldn't welcome a call just now," he said. "You know how busy she is when she's doing a party. We should never interrupt her unless it's an emergency."

Ned resumed reading his paper. Zibby took a shaky breath. There wasn't really anything she could do to help. She tried to tell herself she had no real reason to think her mom needed help in the first place.

She opened her box of stationery and picked up her pen. She began writing a letter to her dad in Italy. She would try to sound cheerful, the way he did in his postcards. But she was feeling anything but cheerful right now.

*Dear Dad (and Sofia),*

*Thanks for all your postcards. Here we have been very busy. Mom's wedding was really nice. I was a bridesmaid. So was Laura-Jane — she is Ned's daughter. He has a little boy, too, named Brady.*

99

*Brady is okay. But Laura-Jane is a monster. I can't stand her.*

*In fact, things have really changed since you left. Mom has been getting tons of terrible headaches. And today somebody wrecked our kitchen. I hope I really can come to Italy SOON.*

Zibby read over what she'd written. It didn't sound especially cheerful after all, she decided. Then, from all the way upstairs in the attic, the sound of banging filtered down to them. Ned lifted his head with a frown. Zibby laid down her pen.

Ned shook his head. "What's Laura-Jane doing up there? She'll wake Brady," he said. "Zibby, would you go to her? See if you can get her to talk to you. I know she's angry at me about the divorce and the wedding and everything. She doesn't want to talk to me. Maybe she'll talk to you."

"I doubt it," said Zibby, reluctant to see Laura-Jane.

"Please?" Ned's eyes crinkled into a smile. "As a favor to your old steppappy?"

"Oh, all *right*," said Zibby. "But she doesn't like me, either." She trudged out of the room and up the stairs, then up the narrow flight to the attic.

Zibby hesitated at the top of the stairs. She peered into Brady's room and saw the little hump of his body under the sheet. Laura-Jane's bedroom door was closed. The banging had stopped.

100

*I could just go away again,* Zibby thought. But she knocked on the door anyway.

"Daddy?" Laura-Jane's voice sounded very small.

"Um, no. It's me. Zibby."

"Go away." Laura-Jane's voice no longer sounded small. It was back to being sullen.

"We heard banging."

Laura-Jane was silent for a long moment. "I was kicking the wall," she rasped.

"Why?"

"Because I felt like it, that's why."

"Oh." Maybe banging made Laura-Jane feel better. "Well, are you all right now?"

"Would you be all right if you were grounded?" hissed Laura-Jane. "Would you be all right if your father loved some other woman better than he did your own mother?"

Sighing, Zibby opened the bedroom door and went inside. Laura-Jane was sitting on her bed, eyes hard, like brilliant black buttons. "Laura-Jane," Zibby began tentatively. "You're right. I'd hate to be grounded. But about your father — about my father, I mean, what you said . . ." She started again. "My dad *does* love another woman better than he loves my mom. Her name is Sofia and she's Italian. I've never even met her."

Laura-Jane sat glaring at Zibby.

"My dad lives in Italy now," Zibby pressed on resolutely. "I haven't seen him for two years. I think you're

101

lucky, you know, because you get to see your dad all the time. *And* your mom. Plus you have Brady. I don't have any brothers or sisters at all." *A couple of ghosts, though,* she thought morosely.

"Well," Laura-Jane said bitterly after a long moment, "now you've got my dad. He's left us and come to you. So I bet you're happy!"

Zibby swallowed a sharp retort. She tried to keep her voice even. It wouldn't help things if she had another fight with Laura-Jane on top of all the other troubles. "I like your dad a lot. And I'm glad he and my mom are happy. But he's not *my* dad. Okay? And it isn't fair of you to say he's left you. You're here, aren't you?"

"Only because I'm grounded!"

"Well, I think it's more that *you've* left *him!*" said Zibby coldly. "Not the other way around."

"I hate him," sobbed Laura-Jane. "I hate everybody."

*And everybody hates you, too,* Zibby thought. But she didn't say it. She sat looking around the little bedroom that Nell and Ned had transformed for this ungrateful girl. It looked cozy and inviting in the glow of the bedside lamp. Laura-Jane's large, pink plastic dollhouse sat on the floor under the window. A breeze through the open window wafted across Zibby's bare arms. Distant thunder rumbled like a giant's footsteps. Zibby thought of giants. To the dolls in the dollhouse, she would be a giant. When Primrose was in the dollhouse, did Zibby look like  giant to her? She would have to ask sometime. If Primrose ever came back.

It didn't seem fair that she had to have Laura-Jane and Miss Honeywell to worry about at once. *Haunted*, she thought. *That's what I am.*

Zibby stood up to leave Laura-Jane alone with her hatreds and moods. But Laura-Jane stopped her with a question. It was asked forcefully, almost spat: "Do you love anyone, Zibby?"

Zibby sat down again. "What do you mean?"

Laura-Jane snorted. "Love? L-O-V-E. You know?"

"Well, I love a lot of people! I love my parents. I love my grandparents. And I suppose I love my cousin Charlotte, even thought she can be a pain —"

"I don't mean *family*, Zibby!" Laura-Jane's voice was scornful. "I mean — boys."

Zibby examined a scab on her knee. She didn't even know where she'd gotten it. "Boys?" she repeated.

"Yes, boys. You know. Males? Young men?" Laura-Jane's voice was sarcastic.

Zibby sighed. Was Laura-Jane going to be like Charlotte — always falling in love and having crushes and talking about boys? Zibby found her cousin's interest in clothes and makeup and males unfathomable. Charlotte said witheringly that Zibby was just too young — although that was ridiculous because the cousins were the same age. Laura-Jane was only ten and a half — almost a full year younger. "No," said Zibby. "I don't love any boys, except maybe Owen. But that's different, because he's family."

"Well, I do." Laura-Jane announced this proudly.

"Good for you." Zibby stood up again. "See you in the morning."

"Don't you want to know who it is?" asked Laura-Jane.

"Not particularly, but I can guess. It's your pizza boy."

"His name is *Todd*. He's the only person I love, besides Brady. Todd is the only person who understands me!" Laura-Jane's voice sounded choked again, and Zibby looked up to see her stepsister's black eyes filled with tears.

"You can't really love him," objected Zibby. "You just met him!"

"He's not the sort who would ever ditch his wife and kids, he told me so," Laura-Jane continued passionately. "He's wonderful and sweet and cute and —"

"He is cute," Zibby agreed. "And nice. Nicer than you, in fact. He helped set up my mom's food at the church hall while you were out riding around being stupid."

Laura-Jane looked startled by this information.

"*But*," continued Zibby, "he's in high school! You're not old enough to date anybody, let alone some guy who's in high school."

"He's not *some guy*, and I'm not dating him. He's just my friend, and I love him." Her black eyes blazed. "It's not fair that Dad says I can't go out all week. How will I see Todd again? I *have* to see him! I have to, and I'm going to."

"Fine. Great." Zibby said. What had Ned sent her

up here for? This whole conversation was stupid. What was she supposed to do? "You should be nicer to your dad," she said for good measure. "And nicer to my mom. It's not her fault your parents got divorced, after all."

"I *hate* your mom," said Laura-Jane. And, horribly, she started to giggle.

"Well I hate *you*! It's your fault my mom's been having so many headaches. You played that she died — and it will be your fault if she really does!" Zibby jumped up and ran out the door. She clattered down the stairs to her own bedroom. Laura-Jane's laughter echoed behind her.

She closed her bedroom door and threw herself across the bed. The breeze from the window was brisker now, and thunder rolled in the distance again. It was going to rain. Zibby was glad. Rain would wash away the humidity, would wash away the oppressive closeness of the room. Rain would clean things up. If only the rain could flood Laura-Jane right out of her life!

Not to mention Miss Honeywell.

Zibby glanced over at the dollhouse. With a sinking feeling in the pit of her stomach, she saw that the mother doll was back in the chimney again.

# Chapter 9

It rained all night. Zibby's sleep was fretful and filled with troubling dreams. Again and again she heard Laura-Jane's horrible laugh and saw her draw her finger suggestively across her neck. Then rollicking music was playing and the bride doll was dancing on top of the wedding cake — holding out her head in her tiny hands like an offering. The mother doll from the dollhouse waved her feet in time to the sprightly music — her head hidden inside the chimney. At last Zibby woke. The room was filled with the rosy light of dawn, but waking did not bring an end to the troubles.

The telephone was ringing.

Zibby peered at her bedside clock and saw it was only 6:20. Who would be calling so early? The ringing broke off and, with some surprise, Zibby heard the low rumble of Ned's voice from the master bedroom. It would take some time before Zibby was used to having a man's voice in the house again.

Suddenly a thought struck her. People only called so early if something were wrong. *Oh, no — not Gram or Gramps!* she thought, and jumped out of bed. She ran into the hall, then into her mom's bedroom. Nell was sitting up in bed next to Ned. Her head was bowed in her hands. Ned replaced the receiver and turned to her. His expression was grave. "It's not poison," he said. "They've learned that much."

"What's happened?" Zibby cried. "Is something wrong with Gram?"

"No, Zibby," said Ned. "That was the hospital calling. Your mom told them to phone us as soon as they knew what was in the food —"

"What food?" cried Zibby. "What are you talking about?"

"The food —" said Nell, now running her hands through her hair as if trying to rub away unpleasant thoughts. "Oh, Zibby, it was a disaster last night."

"What? You mean at the party?"

"That's right." Nell looked up and Zibby saw the deep shadows under her eyes. "Everything was fine after you all left. I served the food, and people were eating and talking and enjoying themselves. Then they had dancing for a couple hours. And then I served the desserts and coffee. You know we had made little lemon tarts, chocolate swirls, cake . . ." Her voice trailed off.

"What happened?" cried Zibby.

"People started gagging. They were spitting out the food and saying it was horrible. They were saying the desserts were poisoned!"

"That's crazy! We made that food ourselves! It was all fresh and —"

"I know," cried Nell. "I know! But something went wrong somewhere. Some of the guests rushed away to the hospital saying they wanted to have their stomachs pumped. Others just went home. The party was ruined — and so is my business!"

"Your mom phoned the police," Ned told Zibby. "They came and took away samples of the food to test them. Then she went to the hospital, and phoned me to come pick her up there. We've hardly had a wink of sleep all night, worrying about everything."

"I told the police to phone me as soon as they had the lab report," Nell said. "They say it wasn't poison in the desserts, thank goodness — but it was something else."

"The police don't think you had anything to do with whatever went wrong, do they?" demanded Zibby, horrified.

"I don't know what they think," sighed Nell, pushing back the sheet. "Though why I'd be trying to put myself out of business, I certainly don't know." She pulled on jeans and a T-shirt, then headed for the stairs.

"I want to come with you," said Zibby. Her thoughts were in a whirl.

"No, honey," Ned said, galloping down the stairs

108

after Nell. "We'll take care of this. You go on back to bed. When Brady and Laura-Jane get up, tell them what's happened. And please make sure Brady gets some breakfast."

Of course Zibby couldn't go back to bed. She watched from the window in her bedroom as Ned's van pulled out of the driveway and swung around the corner, out of sight. She waited at the open window, listening to the morning sounds — the singing of birds and the clanking of garbagemen making their rounds. There was no breeze and the day already felt humid.

Then she sat on the floor near the dollhouse. She ran her hands over the old wood of the roof, reached inside and straightened some of the little furnishings. On a whim, she reached for the old cloth sack that held the little dolls who had come with the house. There were about a dozen or so: mother, father, various children, various servants. Zibby lined up the dolls on the floor and selected a little red-haired girl. She seated the girl in the parlor.

"'This is me,'" she whispered. Then she went to get the little doll with the brown braids — the Primrose doll — from her bedside table. She closed the hinged doors of the house so that the little doll could stand outside on the porch and knock on the front door.

"'Knock, knock,'" she said. And made the red-haired doll inside call out in response, "'Who is it?'"

"'It's me, Primrose Parson,'" she made the Primrose doll answer.

"'Oh, good!'" exclaimed the Zibby doll. "'Please come in.'"

Zibby opened the walls of the house again so that the Primrose doll could come inside. She settled her on the couch in the parlor next to the Zibby doll. "'It's nice to see you again,'" said the red-haired doll. "'Did you have a nice vacation?'"

"'Yes, it was lovely,'" she replied for the Primrose doll. "'But I got tired of being away, and so I hurried back. Are you glad to see me?'"

"'Oh, yes!'" said the Zibby doll fervently. "'It was terrible with you gone. I missed you a lot. And terrible things have been happening. I needed you —'"

*Needed me? Is that past tense?*

The voice in her head made Zibby jump. She grinned with relief. "No, not past tense. Present tense. I *need* you. I need you now, Primrose, and I'm sorry we quarreled. Please come back to the dollhouse. I'll get you the artwork you want. Please come home again."

*Home!* trilled the ghost's little voice. *It sounds nice. And if you're really going to be nice to me and make me some more framed pictures — well, I'll be happy to give it another try. When you and your cousin make me my chandelier, that is. I'm longing for a really elegant chandelier.*

"You'll get it all," Zibby assured her. She reached for the two dolls and brought them out of the house. She laid the red-haired doll on the rug, but held onto the doll with the brown braids. Gently she smoothed the

110

hair. The doll felt slightly weightier now that Primrose's spirit had returned to it.

*But first Miss Honeywell has to leave so I can get back in the dollhouse. She still angry at me, you know. You'd think she would let bygones be bygones, but oh, no, not her.*

In life Primrose Parson and her governess, Miss Calliope Honeywell, had had a very unhappy and troubled relationship. The prim governess tried hard to control the girl by the strictest measures possible, and Primrose retaliated as best she could with practical jokes and mean tricks. One of those practical jokes had backfired tragically — and Miss Honeywell still wanted revenge. That the little girl had grown up, had grown old, had finally died made no difference to the ghost of Miss Honeywell. She still wanted power over her. Primrose had been safe in the dollhouse, as only one ghost at a time could live in it. But by leaving, Primrose had left the door open for Miss Honeywell to enter.

*It may not be so easy to get her out again,* came Primrose's flutey voice in Zibby's head.

"But at least you're here," said Zibby. "Please don't leave. Bad things are happening, and I'm really worried about my mom. Miss Honeywell is trying to hurt her."

*I don't see what I can do though,* said Primrose. *I have enough to worry about trying to stay out of Miss Honeywell's way.*

"But Primrose, when I first agreed to let you live in

my dollhouse, you promised you'd be able to help with things!"

*I meant things like schoolwork. I was very clever when I attended Goodmont Academy, you know. I'm sure my French is still quite fluent and my grasp of algebra —*

"But I don't need help with algebra!" cried Zibby. "I need help protecting my mom from your horrible, evil governess!"

*It's not so easy.* The little voice seemed to sigh in Zibby's head. *You don't understand.*

That was true. Zibby *didn't* understand how ghosts spent their time. And so far Primrose had not been very forthcoming when asked. "No artwork," Zibby said succinctly, "and no chandelier if you won't try to help."

*I'll try! I said I would try. I just can't promise anything.* The ghost's reedy voice held a note of entreaty. Zibby realized with a start that Primrose was still afraid of the governess.

"All right," Zibby said. "Thank you."

"Oh, no, not only do I have to live with my dad's home-wrecking wife, I've got to put up with her lunatic daughter, too!" Laura-Jane's sarcastic voice from the bedroom doorway made Zibby turn with a start. "Talking to dolls!" She stepped into the room. "Here, I know a really good game we can play — about how the mom doll pretends to be Santa Claus and gets her head stuck in the chimney! Poor dear, she didn't know there was a fire lit below. In no time at all, she's suffocated!"

Zibby jumped up, still holding the little Primrose doll. "You think you're just being funny with your mean games," she shouted, "but you don't know what Miss Honeywell can do! It will be your fault if my mom really gets hurt!"

Laura-Jane smirked. "Miss Honey-*who*?"

"Just get out of here. Don't come in my room at all. And don't you dare touch the dollhouse again." Zibby started toward her. "Out!"

Laura-Jane backed out into the hall. "Okay, okay! Keep your head on!"

Brady's small figure emerged from the master bedroom. "What are you fighting about?" he asked in a scared voice. "Where's Dad? I can't find Dad."

Zibby remembered that Laura-Jane and Brady didn't know about the food poisoning. She laid the doll on her bedside table, then turned to her stepsister and stepbrother. "Let's go downstairs, and I'll tell you what's going on." She pulled the door to her room firmly closed behind them and started down the stairs. "As much as I know about what's going on, anyway."

Laura-Jane and Brady followed her. They sat at the kitchen table and ate their breakfasts. Zibby told them about the phone call.

"Food poison!" rasped Laura-Jane. She poured milk over her cereal and stirred it around energetically. "That's bad for business, I bet. I mean, who wants to hire a caterer who puts stuff into the food that makes people sick?"

113

Zibby stared at her angrily. "My mom didn't put anything in the food! And it wasn't poison anyway."

"You mean there was spoiled meat or something?" asked Brady.

"I don't know. It seemed to be in the desserts, Mom said. Some of the people got scared and went to have their stomachs pumped at the hospital."

"Someone might die," Brady announced importantly. "I saw a show on TV about people who ate bad meat and died. Maybe some of those people in the hospital will die, too."

Laura-Jane grew still. She laid her spoon on the table. "I don't think so, Brady. It's not that serious."

"But if anyone *did* die, my mom would be responsible." The thought made Zibby feel dizzy. She pushed her bowl of cereal away, uneaten. "My mom could end up in prison — for murder! Bet that would make you happy, wouldn't it, Laura-Jane?"

Laura-Jane didn't answer. She looked a bit dizzy herself.

# Chapter 10

The phone rang. Zibby sprang to answer. She was expecting her mom or Ned, but Todd's deep voice asked politely for Laura-Jane. Zibby handed over the phone. "Don't talk long," she ordered her stepsister. "We might get a call from the hospital."

Laura-Jane grabbed the receiver and hunched over it, speaking in a low voice. Brady ambled out of the room. In another moment Zibby could hear the sound of Laura-Jane's muttering right there in the kitchen.

"Yes," Laura-Jane murmured into the phone. "I know. Well, you didn't tell me — well, okay. Okay. No, no, I don't think so." A furtive look at Zibby. "Well, no. But maybe here instead." After listening another minute she spoke again. "Great! See you soon."

She hung up. Zibby crossed her arms. "Don't forget that you're grounded."

"You're not my boss, Zibby Thorne!" yelled Laura-Jane.

"No, but —"

"And for your information, Todd is coming *here*. Dad didn't say anything about not seeing friends here, did he?" Laura-Jane shook back her straight, dark hair and stuck out her tongue. "So there!" She ran out of the kitchen and Zibby heard the thud of her feet on the stairs.

Zibby was glad Todd was coming over. He would be able to keep Laura-Jane out of her way. He might even be able to talk to her about how horribly she was acting. Since Laura-Jane hero-worshipped him, she might listen to him.

Zibby phoned Jude. Her friend gasped when she heard about the ruined food and the police. "This is awful!" she cried. "How are the police going to catch a ghost?"

"Exactly," Zibby said. "That's what I was thinking, too. But, Jude, at least we might have some help. Primrose Parson has come back!"

"She has! When? How?"

Zibby told her friend about her earlier conversation with the ghost. "She won't go back into the house, though. She senses that Miss Honeywell is around."

"We sense that, too," mused Jude. "In a big way."

"I don't understand how it works with ghosts," complained Zibby. "All this 'sensing.' You'd think once you were dead, you'd get over whatever problems you had in your lifetime."

"Well, maybe most people do," said Jude. "But not

these two. Anyway, we'd better have a club meeting. I'll call Charlotte and we can meet at the tree —"

"No, you'd better come here instead. I'm supposed to be watching Brady."

"Okay. And maybe we can get Primrose talking to us. She might know what we can do to get rid of Miss Honeywell. Your mom has had so many close calls lately, it's not funny."

"You can say that again," said Zibby forcefully.

The front doorbell rang. "I'll get it!" screeched Brady, and Zibby heard his footsteps running from the living room into the hallway.

"No, I'll get it! It's for me!" yelled Laura-Jane, pounding down the stairs.

"I've gotta go," Zibby told Jude. "But come over as soon as you can."

In the hallway, Brady and Laura-Jane had collided. Brady was sobbing, rubbing his elbow. "She hit me on the funny bone," he cried. "But it doesn't feel very funny!"

"Sorry!" snapped Laura-Jane, "but you shouldn't get in the way." Then she opened the screen door and her face broke into a wide smile. When she spoke, her voice had changed from snappy to sweet. "Hi Todd!"

"Good morning, everybody." Todd stepped inside. "Hey, buddy, let's see that elbow."

Brady held out his arm, sniffing tearfully.

Todd inspected it carefully. "I think it'll be okay, but

just to be sure, we'd better put some of this magic powder on it." Brady watched, fascinated, as Todd rooted around in his back pocket. "Here we go."

Todd held a little paper packet in his hand. Zibby saw it was a tiny packet of sugar from the Pizza Den. Todd ripped it open and sprinkled the sugar into his palm. He lifted Brady's elbow and sprinkled the sugar over the injury. "There you go! All fixed up and rarin' to go."

Brady's face was transformed by his wide grin. "Hey, yeah! It feels all better! Hey, Todd, wanna come up and jump on my bed? It's not as good as your trampoline, but I can nearly touch the ceiling!"

"Some other time, buddy." Todd smiled at the girls. "He's really got the bug, doesn't he? The acrobat bug."

"Well, your trampoline was so cool, Todd," gushed Laura-Jane. "I loved it, too. And the tricks you can do! They're amazing. Even High-and-Mighty Miss Zibby would be impressed. Come on, show Zibby."

Todd slanted Zibby a smile. "Want to see a back flip?"

Zibby smiled back. "Sure. Why not?" She liked the way he'd used the magic powder to cheer Brady up, and she liked the way Laura-Jane brightened in his presence. She felt a bit brighter herself when he was around. She hoped to get him alone while he was here today and tell him about Laura-Jane's unhappiness and meanness, and ask his help with her stepsister. She wouldn't reveal what Laura-Jane had said about loving him, of course.

Todd clapped his hands together briskly. "All right then, ladies and gentlemen, stand well back. Give the man some room!"

Brady, Laura-Jane, and Zibby moved into the doorway of the dining room. In a flash, Todd jumped into the air, twisted himself head over heels and landed gracefully on his feet. "That's a single," he said, grinning at their expressions. "I'm working on a double," he told them, "but I haven't got it down yet."

"Yes you do," cried Laura-Jane. "On the trampoline!"

"True," Todd said. "But acrobats can't rely on the trampoline all the time."

"So is that what you want to be?" asked Zibby. "An acrobat?"

"I *am* an acrobat," corrected Todd. "Like my mother. She joined the circus when I was only a little kid. The flying lady!" He saw her bemused expression and laughed. "Think I'm kidding, hmm? Well, I'm not. It's true. My mother is in Germany or someplace now, flying through the air with the greatest of ease. She's a trapeze artist."

"And you're going to join the circus, too, aren't you, Todd?" asked Laura-Jane eagerly. She stepped up and took his arm. "And we'll come watch you. You'll be famous!"

Todd grinned. "My biggest fan," he told Zibby.

"I'm your fan, too!" cried Brady.

*Me, too*, thought Zibby, dazzled.

Todd gently disengaged himself from Laura-Jane's grasp. "I'll get you free tickets when I'm star of the show, okay?"

"Okay!" Brady stood there for another minute, obviously hoping Todd would spring into action again. But when he didn't, Brady sloped off to watch television. Ned was fairly strict about the amount of television he allowed his children to watch, and Brady tried to sneak in a few extra shows whenever he could.

"So, L-J," Todd was saying. "How about we go outside and I'll tell you about what life under the big top will be like?"

"Yes," said Laura-Jane shyly. "Tell me about your mom, and how she's waiting for you to join her!" Then she frowned at Zibby. "Don't look so mean, Zibby. I'm just going out on the porch."

"She's grounded," Zibby told Todd. "She has to stay home. Her dad said."

Laura-Jane flushed.

"We'll stay put," he promised. "I'll look after her."

Zibby watched them go out the front door. The screen slammed behind them. She wandered aimlessly back to the kitchen. She couldn't understand what Todd saw in a little kid like Laura-Jane. Her cousin Owen was fifteen, but he seemed a world away. He wouldn't be caught dead hanging out with Charlotte

120

and her friends. Still, it was nice for Laura-Jane that she had found a big-brother figure in Todd to keep her out of trouble. Zibby wouldn't mind having him as *her* minder, actually, she reflected with a sigh. Now if only Miss Honeywell could find a friend to keep *her* out of trouble!

Then Jude and Penny arrived. The girls went upstairs to Zibby's room and sat in front of the old dollhouse to wait for Charlotte. *It shouldn't take Charlotte long to whizz across town on her fancy bike*, Zibby reflected. Then the four of them would have to put their heads together and come up with some way to stop Miss Honeywell from threatening Nell anymore. "It's all Laura-Jane's fault that Miss Honeywell is threatening my mom," Zibby reminded the others. "Because she's the one who, you know, *invoked* Miss Honeywell by playing that mean game about the bride."

"That's true," said fair-minded Jude, "but you have to remember that Laura-Jane doesn't know what she did. She's just trying to be mean to you — she doesn't know about Miss Honeywell."

"In fact," piped up Penny, "all the trouble really started because Zibby had the fight with Primrose. Primrose got mad and went away — and *that* left the door open for horrible Miss Honeywell."

"Great," muttered Zibby. "So now it's all *my* fault."

"No — it's Primrose's fault for going away," said Penny. "That's what I meant, really."

They looked up as they heard footsteps clattering

121

up the stairs. Charlotte sauntered into the bedroom. "I think after what happened yesterday you would at least keep your doors locked," she greeted Zibby. "Anybody can just walk right in!"

"But Laura-Jane's out on the porch —" said Zibby.

"No she's not," said Charlotte.

Zibby frowned. "She should be. She was sitting on the swing with Todd."

"Well," replied Charlotte. "She's not there now. So I just let myself in. Anyway, what's all this about the poisoned food, Zibby? Jude said I should get over here quick — and I raced liked the wind." She shook back her mane of long, blonde hair. "I've got a zillion tangles now, and it's your fault."

"Everything's my fault," Zibby said dolefully. She got up and went to the doorway. "Laura-Jane?" she yelled. She walked out into the hallway and stood at the foot of the attic steps. "Laura-Jane? Are you up there?"

No answer. Leaving Jude and Penny to give Charlotte the details about the poisoned food, Zibby climbed the steps and looked into Laura-Jane's bedroom. The bed was neatly made. But Laura-Jane wasn't there. Zibby looked into Brady's room but that, too, was empty. She ran back down the stairs, past the other club members peering out from her bedroom doorway, and ran on down into the front hall. The television in the living room was off. "Brady?" she called.

122

No answer. Zibby stepped outside onto the front porch. "Laura-Jane?" Nothing.

Then Zibby notice that Todd's bike was gone. So was Laura-Jane's. "I can't believe this," she moaned.

"What's going on, Zib?" Jude had come down the stairs after her.

"It looks like Todd and Laura-Jane rode off some-where — and they've taken Brady, too!"

"But where would they go?"

"Well, Brady was begging earlier to go to Todd's house to play on the trampoline. I guess they might have gone there. But Laura-Jane knows she's supposed to stay home!"

"It's not your fault," said Jude. "It's not like you're her baby-sitter."

"I feel like I am these days," muttered Zibby. Life she reflected, had certainly been easier when she and her mom lived alone. "But I feel I should be watching out for Brady."

She and Jude went back upstairs to Penny and Charlotte. They were talking about the food. "Zibby's mom and Ned are at the police station now, trying to figure out who could have done it," said Penny.

"It's not like the cops are ever going to catch Miss Honeywell!" Charlotte shook her head.

"I know. So that leaves it up to us."

"And to Primrose," Zibby said. She looked out the window, hoping to see Brady and Laura-Jane.

"Has Primrose come back?" asked Charlotte.

"Yes." Zibby turned away from the window. "And Primrose wants to get rid of Miss Honeywell, too. She can't move back into the dollhouse as long as Miss Honeywell is there."

"Where is she, then?" asked Penny.

Zibby pointed to the little doll propped on her bedside table.

"Poor Primrose!" exclaimed Penny, going over and picking up the doll. "Are you homeless, poor thing? I wish I had a dollhouse. If I did, I'd let you live in it."

"What, and leave me with Miss Honeywell? No way," said Zibby.

"Zibby and I are going to build you a house for your birthday, but that's not for months," Jude reminded her. "Anyway, why can't we just put the Primrose doll in the house and leave her there?"

"Primrose's spirit won't stay in the doll until Miss Honeywell is gone," replied Zibby. "She's afraid of Miss Honeywell."

"Maybe she'd stay if we made her some new things for the rooms?" asked Charlotte. "I know I always like my room better when it's got some new posters up on the walls, or a new quilt on my bed."

Zibby shook her head. "She told me she won't live there until Miss Honeywell is gone. But I did promise we'll make her some new things for the house. Since she's going to help us."

"Let's start right now," urged Penny. "Get those

stamps that she wanted, and we can make a couple of frames."

"Might as well," Zibby went to her desk and brought over the box of postcards. The girls searched among them for the prettiest stamps, then carefully peeled them off the stiff cards. They got out the art supplies again and began making frames as before. As they started working, Zibby brought the little doll over and set her on the floor near their supplies.

"Okay, Primrose," began Zibby. "How can we scare Miss Honeywell out of the dollhouse and back into the great beyond — where she can't make trouble?" She reached out her hands to Charlotte and Jude. Penny held onto Jude's arm. This way they could all hear Primrose's reply.

*There's no scaring that one away, you should know that by now.* Primrose's little voice held a hopeless note.

The slam of the van door out in the driveway sent the girls running to the window. The little doll was left propped against the shoe box of postcards. Ned and Nell walked up the porch steps. "I'd better go down," Zibby said reluctantly. "And tell them that Laura-Jane and Brady are gone."

"We'll wait for you," Charlotte assured her. "We can listen to the fireworks from here."

Zibby tossed her head. "Thanks for your moral support!"

She went downstairs. Her mom and Ned had come

into the house and collapsed in the living room. Zibby sat hesitantly next to Nell on the couch. "So, what's happening? What did the police say? Are the people who ate the desserts okay?"

Nell nodded. "It wasn't poison, as you've already heard. It was soap! Industrial strength, lemon cleanser with some pretty harsh ingredients, but nothing that would kill you, thank goodness."

"It was in the whipped cream," said Ned. "Stirred right in."

"The whipped cream was in the big blue bowl," Zibby remembered. "I carried it in from the van myself."

"Did you taste it?" asked Ned.

"No. It had plastic wrap over it, and I just left it on the counter."

"And then I put it into the refrigerator. Later I took the wrapper off and spread the cream onto the cakes and tarts," said Nell. "I didn't taste it either. So there was about an hour and a half that it was in the fridge — and anyone could have messed with it."

"So what are the police doing?" asked Zibby.

"Oh, they're conducting an investigation. It's a popular brand of soap, apparently. The sort used in schools and restaurants and hotels. The police are checking which places around town use it or sell it. But I'm not sure that will really tell them anything." She rubbed her tired, red-rimmed eyes. "I don't know, Zibby. I must just be having a run of bad luck. First someone sabotages the party food in the kitchen. Then some joker spikes the whipped cream. It's hard to believe the incidents can be related."

"I think they *are* related," said Ned. "Someone is afraid of you. Someone wants you out of business. That's what the police need to look into. Which caterers in town are jealous that you've managed to do so well? Who is trying to start a catering company and wants to get rid of the stiffest competition? Who just happened to be walking past us when we were setting up the food?"

"The Ballantynes — I know that's what you're getting at. But there's room for more than one caterer even in a small town like this. Why would they need to hurt me?" Nell shook her head.

Zibby bit her lip. The Ballantynes were creepy people, and she wished she could pin this trouble on them. But it was more complicated than that. It was Laura-Jane who had set Nell up as the target without even knowing what she was doing. By acting out the dead bride game with the dollhouse dolls, Laura-Jane had given Miss Honeywell that pattern for her horrid play.

"Laura-Jane and Brady are gone," she announced abruptly. She'd rather see her mom and Ned angry at Laura-Jane than worrying about Nell's catering company. At least there was a chance they could do something about Laura-Jane. She could be caught and brought home and locked in her room. But there was no easy way to catch a ghost, no easy way to make *her* stop.

"Gone?" roared Ned. "Gone where?"

"I — I don't know," stammered Zibby. Maybe it wasn't better having them angry at Laura-Jane after all.

"But she's grounded," said Nell. "I thought you'd made that perfectly clear, Ned."

"Oh, she understood it," Zibby hastened to explain. "And when Todd came over, I even reminded them. They were just sitting on the porch swing, talking, and Brady was watching cartoons, and I went upstairs. Jude and Penny and Charlotte came over. We were just making stuff for my dollhouse . . ."

"I'll go check Todd's house right now," said Ned, standing up and reaching for his keys on the mantel. "Where does he live? Do you know?"

"I don't know," admitted Zibby.

"His last name is Parkfield," Nell said, also standing up. "Maybe his address will be in the phone book, dear."

Ned stomped to the kitchen to check. Nell met Zibby's eyes.

"Oh, Mom." Zibby heard the helpless note in her voice. "I'm sorry. I should have been watching Brady. I didn't think he'd leave!"

"You weren't the only one who was supposed to be watching Brady," said Nell. "Laura-Jane knew very well she wasn't supposed to leave, much less take him with her."

"I'm just not used to looking after little kids," Zibby admitted. "If anything has happened to him —"

"I'm sure he's fine," Nell said softly. "Don't worry, honey. Things will settle down. It's hard on Laura-Jane and Brady, moving in with us. They probably just need time to get used to us, to the house, and to the neighborhood. In fact, maybe that's what they're doing now. Maybe they didn't go to Todd's house at all — they could just be biking around or playing in the park."

Ned returned with Todd's address written on a slip of paper. "I phoned, but there was no answer," he said. "So I'm going to drive on over."

Nell ran her hands through her long hair and quickly spun it up into a knot on the top of her head. She secured the knot with an elastic band she pulled from the pocket of her jeans. "Whew, it's hot," she said. "But I'm going to walk down to check the park now." She tucked her keys into her pocket, along with her slim billfold. "Who knows, maybe I'll find Laura-Jane and Brady at the playground. I'll treat them to an ice cream and try to initiate peace talks!"

Ned kissed the tip of her nose. "I'm sorry, darling, that my kids are giving you all this trouble. I'm glad Zibby doesn't go on the warpath."

Nell hugged Zibby. "Oh, she has her moments, don't you, sweetheart? But we muddle along, and that's what we'll keep on doing."

Zibby watched them go out the door, marveling at the way they leaped from one problem to the other, working together, taking things in stride. They made a good team, she reflected. Her dad, on the other hand, wasn't the sort who worked as part of a team. He liked to make decisions and act on them without consulting others. Maybe Sofia could deal with that better than Nell had.

She went into the kitchen, thinking about the nature of parents, and prepared a snack to take upstairs to the others. Some ripe peaches in a bowl, some wedges of cheese, and a box of wheat crackers. These she carried with her as she climbed the stairs back to her bedroom.

The good parents, it seemed to her, were the kind who put their own troubles aside when their children needed them — even when the children were idiots like Laura-Jane, who didn't deserve the attention. The bad parents were the kind who selfishly put their own interests and needs first. Laura-Jane and Brady, Charlotte and Penny and Jude all had the first kind, the kind she had herself. Primrose Parson, Zibby remembered, had had the second kind of parents. They had seemed kind and friendly, and showered Primrose with a virtual toyshop of toys, but in the end they'd left her with Miss Honeywell. And that's when things started going wrong — wrong for Primrose, and wrong for Zibby — and now wrong for Nell.

*Always blaming someone else,* came Primrose's accusing voice in Zibby's head. *So now you think it's my parents' fault that Miss Honeywell is making trouble for your mother? I don't*

130

*like that, Zibby. Miss Honeywell is a bad one, I'll grant you that. But there's more going on around here than meets the eye.*

"What do you mean, Primrose?" demanded Zibby, stopping at the top of the stairs. "What eye?"

But before Primrose could answer, the screen door banged and the sound of crying filled the hallway. But the cries were not Laura-Jane's, as Zibby might have expected. They were Nell's.

"Mom! What is it?" Zibby turned and raced down the stairs.

Nell lurched into the hall, then stopped and stared up at Zibby, wide-eyed. She seemed unable to speak, could only sob, her breath coming in short, wrenching gasps. Zibby felt fingers of fear tighten around her. Something very bad had happened, and Zibby was almost afraid to learn what it was.

Nell's hair had been wrenched from its bun on the top of her head. It hung in tangles around her smudged, bruised face. Her hands were covered in dirt. And, Zibby was horrified to see, there was something else—red stuff smeared across her mom's cheek and dripping down her chin onto her neck. . . . Zibby blinked, hugging the bowl of peaches, the cheese and crackers to her chest. She willed the red stuff to be ketchup—or paint. She willed it to vanish. But it didn't—and it wasn't ketchup, wasn't paint. It was blood.

# Chapter 11

"Mom—" moaned Zibby. She hurtled down the stairs. "Oh, Mom, you're *hurt!*"

Nell staggered against her. She put out a dirt-smeared hand and gripped the newel post. She lowered herself to sit on the bottom step. "Don't panic," she murmured, and it seemed as much an order to herself as to Zibby. "Don't panic. Everything will be all right."

"No, it won't be!" cried Zibby. "Look at you! What happened?" But it was all too clear that her mom had been attacked.

"What happened?" echoed the voices of Charlotte, Jude, and Penny as they came out of Zibby's room and peered down the stairs.

"Quick, somebody — get a towel from the bathroom!" Zibby barked the order, and Charlotte gasped. She turned and ran down the hall. She returned in a moment and tossed the towel down to Zibby. Zibby caught it. She knelt over her mom. "Here, put this around your neck. There's all that blood —" She had to look away. The streaks of blood made her dizzy.

Jude came down the stairs and gently moved Zibby aside. She sat next to Nell. "Let me see," she said calmly.

Nell was sitting with her head bowed and her eyes closed but she lifted her head so Jude could see the blood.

"It looks bad, but I'm pretty sure it's just a heavy nosebleed," Jude diagnosed after a moment. "Zibby, it's okay." She put her hand tentatively on Nell's bowed shoulder. "You'll be okay."

"Jude ought to be a doctor," Penny said proudly. "That's what my mom and dad say. Like Mac and Sarah."

"Just because my parents are doctors doesn't mean I'm going to be," said Jude as she tipped Nell's head back and stanched the blood with the towel. "I'm going to be an architect. Hey, Penny, go get some frozen vegetables from their freezer, will you?"

Penny hurried off obligingly.

"Vegetables?" Zibby stared at her friend. It seemed an odd moment to get a craving. "Can't you wait for lunchtime?"

Charlotte frowned. "I don't think Aunt Nell feels like eating right now."

Jude laughed. "Not to eat! To put on her forehead — cold is a great way to stop nosebleeds. My dad showed me. It doesn't have to be vegetables, either — but a bag of frozen vegetables will be easier for her to hold on her forehead than a bunch of ice cubes."

Penny returned with some frozen peas. Jude pressed the cold bag to Nell's forehead. "There you go," Jude said. "That should stop the blood in a second."

And it did. Zibby, Charlotte, and Penny applauded when, after another few minutes, Nell removed the bag and the towel and looked at Jude. "Thank you," she said faintly. She looked at the other girls. "Thank you all."

"Mom — what *happened?*"

Nell shook her head, then groaned and pushed the peas against her forehead again. Zibby heard the chug of Ned's van outside in the driveway, then the slam of the heavy doors. Footsteps clattered on the porch outside. Zibby ran to the door.

"Oh, Ned, hurry!"

Ned stepped into the house, closely followed by Brady.

Ned stopped. "Nell!" He ran to her. "Oh, no, what now?"

"She'll be all right," Jude told him. "At least, I think so."

Brady sidled over, looking scared. "Is that red stuff on the towel *blood?*" he asked in an awed voice.

"I was mugged in the park, if you can believe it," said Nell softly. "Oh, Ned, right here in our park! Of all places — I always felt Carroway was the safest place in the world to live."

Ned was checking the nosebleed. "Good doctoring job," he said tightly.

"That was Jude," said Zibby. "She knew what to do."

"She ought to be a doctor," Penny insisted. "But she —"

"Ssh!" exclaimed Jude, brushing aside Penny's praise. "Let's hear what happened."

"I went to the park to look for Laura-Jane and Brady," began Nell in a low voice. She raised her head painfully and peered at Brady. "There *you* are, Brady. But where is your sister?"

"She's in the van," Ned said in a tight voice. "Sulking. But forget her for now. Tell me what happened to you."

Nell closed her eyes as if the sunlight spilling into the hallway through the open door made them hurt. "I had just reached the park," she murmured, "and was heading on the path toward the playground. Then suddenly someone grabbed me around the neck — grabbed me from behind! Oh, Ned, I've never been so frightened in my life. Whoever it was was stronger, and taller than me. He hissed into my ear, 'don't scream or you've had it!' and then threw me into the bushes. He kept his knee on my back so I couldn't turn over, and I felt him ripping my wallet out of my pocket. Then he pushed my face down into the dirt — hard. When I finally managed to get up, my nose was pouring blood, and he was gone."

"*He?* Are you sure it was a man?" asked Zibby. Miss Honeywell might not have been a particularly strong woman when she was alive. But as a ghost, Miss Honeywell could no doubt summon unearthly strength.

Nell looked at her in some surprise. "I didn't see whoever it was. But I thought, I mean — yes, I thought it was a man."

"When he told her not to scream, she could probably tell," said Charlotte.

"Yeah, but if the voice was *hissing*," Zibby argued, "you might not be able to tell."

"*Don't scream,*" hissed Brady experimentally. He looked up at his dad. "Could you tell I'm a man?"

They all had to laugh, though Nell's laugh was still shaky. "Oh, Brady," she said. "You would never hiss at anyone from the bushes, would you?"

"Nope," he said. He looked at her intently. "Those peas are going all melty."

She held the bag of frozen peas away from her head and looked at it. "So they are." She seemed to recover her usual calm. "We'll have to eat them tonight for supper."

Ned helped her to her feet and looked her over. "Nothing broken?"

She shook her limbs. "No, only scratches. I think I'm more dirty and shocked than hurt."

"Thank goodness for that." Ned hugged her. "Why don't you go up and take a shower while I phone the police — no, on second thought, better not take a shower yet. The police ought to see you as you look now. See what damage that creep did."

"Did you lose a lot of money?" asked Jude sympathetically.

"Oh — not in cash. Only about ten dollars, I think, and some change," Nell answered. She rubbed her scraped arms ruefully. "But of course there's my driver's license, and my bank card — and the wallet itself. It was a birthday gift from Zibby and I treasured it."

"Don't worry, Mom, I'll get you another one," said Zibby staunchly. But she was sorry the wallet had been stolen. She had saved her money and chosen it carefully. It was supple black leather with top stitching in a golden thread. The stitching formed a pattern of daisies, the flower symbol of DaisyCakes. Zibby had been so excited when she'd seen it by chance one day at a department store in Columbus, and she'd asked the clerk to hold it for her until she could return with her money. It was the perfect gift for Nell, and now it was gone.

The screen door opened and Laura-Jane sidled inside. "There you are," said Ned ominously. "I think you owe your stepmother an apology."

"What for?" muttered Laura-Jane. Then she looked at Nell and grew pale. She looked away again.

"*This* is what happened to Nell when she went out searching for you and Brady, young lady! If you had stayed home where you were supposed to be, this wouldn't have happened."

"But, Dad —" Laura-Jane darted another glance at Nell.

"Don't blame her, Ned," objected Nell. "It isn't her fault there was a mugger lurking in the park. Where did you find the kids, anyway?"

"She and Brady were riding their bikes over by the high school. Brady was good enough to tell me they had gone to watch Todd's gymnastic practice in the school gym. Laura-Jane, I'm sorry to say, pleaded the Fifth Amendment."

"What's that?" Penny whispered. Zibby was wondering the same thing.

But Jude knew. "It's part of the Constitution. It gives you a legal right to remain silent if what you're going to say could get you in trouble."

"It was so cool!" said Brady, his eyes shining. "You should see the way Todd can jump. He's going to try out for the gymnastic team when school starts, he told us. I want to be a gymnast, too, Dad. Can I? Please, can I?"

"They were on their way home, with Brady on the back of Laura-Jane's bike," Ned continued without answering Brady's excited questions. "Laura-Jane claims to have forgotten she was grounded. I pitched the bike into the van and drove them back." He turned to look at Laura-Jane. "You're grounded an extra week now. Let's not have any more of this sort of behavior. It's a shame to spend the rest of your summer vacation cooped up at home instead of out making friends. But unless your attitude improves, home is where you'll be."

Laura-Jane's cheeks flushed crimson. She pushed past the girls at the bottom of the stairs and stomped up to her room without a single word.

Nell stood up carefully. "Well," she sighed, "so far this is a day I could have done without — and it's not even lunchtime." She looked at the girls and Brady all gathered around her. "Let's go call the police and you girls can make us some sandwiches. If things are going to go on this way, we'll need some sustenance."

"I'll call the police," Ned said. "The mugger is probably long gone, but who knows? He might be hanging around waiting to jump on someone else."

"Tell the police to hurry," Nell pleaded, holding out her blood-smeared hands. "Tell them I need to take a nice long shower."

The police arrived quickly. Zibby, Charlotte, Jude, and Penny hovered near the windows in the living room while Nell and Ned talked to the two officers. As on their first visit, Officer Grayling took careful notes.

"Third call in two days," Officer Marec stated. "The kitchen was vandalized, the food had soap powder in it, and now you've been attacked and robbed. You've been having a hard time, haven't you, ma'am?"

Nell laughed shortly. "That's putting it mildly. I'm beginning to feel paranoid."

Officer Grayling looked grave. "You may be right to feel in danger," she said seriously. "Each of these

139

crimes seems to be aimed at you directly. Do you have any idea who could be behind them?"

"Anyone who is angry at you?" prompted the male officer. "Who wants to hurt you?"

Nell frowned and glanced at Ned. Zibby suspected they were thinking of Hilda and Hector Ballantyne. The rival caterers in town *would* be the logical suspects — if you didn't know about Miss Honeywell.

But Nell shook her head. "No, not really," she told the police officers. "I do compete with other catering firms in the area for people's business. But I can't believe any one of them would sink so low — or be so desperate — as to try to sabotage DaisyCakes or to injure me."

"Well, we'd like you to give us the names of the other firms so that we can check on them," said the male officer decisively. "You never know."

"I hate to get anyone in trouble —" began Nell uncertainly, but Ned interrupted.

"If they haven't done anything wrong, then they won't be in trouble!"

"True enough," agreed Nell. She gave the police the names of Hilda and Hector Ballantyne, Jean Godfrey, and Bethellen Muldoon. "Bethellen and Jean both work in Fennel Grove, but the other two are right here in town."

"Thank you very much," said Officer Marec. "We'll get straight to work on this and will report back as soon as we have any word." He gave them a confident smile.

"In the meantime," added Officer Grayling, "be extra careful. Expect the unexpected."

Then they were gone, and Zibby stared after them thoughtfully. *Expect the unexpected,* she thought. The words reminded her of Primrose's comment earlier that there was more going on around here than met the eye.

Nell went upstairs to wash off the dirt and put antiseptic on her scrapes. Ned climbed the stairs to Laura-Jane's attic bedroom. Brady saw the children across the street outside in their yard, watching the police car drive away. He rushed out to impress them with details of the morning's events. Zibby turned to the other girls, who had been sitting on the couch in the living room listening silently to the adults' conversation.

"I know the police are going to try to help," she said slowly, "but I don't think they're going to get very far."

"No," agreed Jude. "I was thinking the same thing."

"We could try to tell them about Miss Honeywell," began Penny, but Charlotte's snort of derision interrupted her.

"Come *on*, Penny! We've been through this already. Do you think the police are going to listen for one second to a bunch of girls who come in talking about ghosts in a dollhouse?" Charlotte tossed back her long blonde hair disdainfully. "Don't be so childish."

"I'm just trying to help," snapped Penny. "I'm worried about Zibby's mom, even if you're not. I remember what Miss Honeywell can do, even if you don't. Remember — my own brother nearly died because of Miss Honeywell!" Her voice rose angrily.

"Okay, okay," Jude said hastily, shooting Charlotte an annoyed look. She was quick to tease and taunt her young aunt herself, but rallied to Penny's defense if anyone else seemed unkind. And Charlotte could annoy them all with her sometimes superior manner. "Calm down! We're *all* worried about Zibby's mom. We *all* remember what Miss Honeywell can do. Fighting isn't going to stop the ghost or help anybody."

"Let's go to the clubhouse," suggested Zibby. "We can talk about what to do next. I mean, Charlotte's right — the police won't believe a word about ghosts. They're going to be busy checking on the other caterers in town and won't be a step closer to protecting my mom. So it's up to *us* to figure things out."

"That's what I was trying to say in the first place," Charlotte pointed out. "The police aren't going to stop the trouble. But maybe we can."

"That's what I was going to say, too," Penny said plaintively. "If anyone would let me talk around here! I was saying we could try to tell them about Miss Honeywell, but they probably wouldn't listen! So what we need to do is work all together to protect Zibby's mom — *and* we need to get Primrose working on a way to get rid of that governess ghost. She's a

142

ghost herself, so she should know better than us what to do."

"So then we all agree," said Zibby. She ran upstairs quickly to get the little Primrose doll from her bedroom. Then she stopped to call to her mom over the noise of the shower that she would be at Jude and Penny's.

The shower stopped. "Would you like to take Laura-Jane along?" Nell asked through the bathroom door.

Zibby snorted. "You're kidding, right, Mom?"

"Actually, I'm not. I know she's grounded, but she's also at loose ends. I think that's part of her trouble. At her mom's house, she has friends in the neighborhood. Here — she hasn't made friends."

"And she never will if she keeps acting so horrible," said Zibby.

There was silence for a moment, then Nell's voice came softly again through the closed door. "All right, honey. Maybe next time."

Zibby frowned at the door. *Don't hold your breath,* she almost snapped. But the thought of her mom's breath made Zibby pause. In and out, in and out, went Nell's breathing. It was the regular rhythm of life, but so often taken for granted — until something happened as a reminder of how fragile life is, and how precious. The beheaded bride doll from the cake flashed in Zibby's memory and made her speak gently. "Mom? Be careful, okay? Don't, um, slip in the shower and hit your head — or anything like that."

"I'll be careful, honey," came Nell's reply. The pulsing *whoosh* of the shower resumed.

Zibby ran back down to the girls who waited in the hallway. "Let's go," she said, leading the way out of the house. "Who knows how much time we have before Miss Honeywell strikes again?"

# Chapter 12

The club members sat under the bower of leaves and tried to figure out a plan.

"Let's make a list," suggested practical Jude, taking her tiny spiral notebook from its hiding place among the tree roots. "What has Miss Honeywell done to Zibby's mom so far?"

"Well, first she made the bride's head fall off," said Penny. "On the cake."

"Wait a sec," objected Charlotte. "That might have been Miss Honeywell's doing, but it didn't actually hurt anybody. It just happened. We'd better focus on the ways Miss Honeywell has actually hurt Aunt Nell."

"The tires," said Zibby promptly. "Someone punctured all four tires on Ned's car. They could have had a bad accident. But even so, it was a mean thing to do, and a big inconvenience."

"Tires," said Jude, writing it down.

"Well, then there was the kitchen mess," said Penny.

She glanced at Charlotte as if to dare the other girl to deny this one.

"Right," said Charlotte, flashing Penny her perfect smile.

Penny looked gratified. "And then there was the poisoned food."

"But it wasn't poison," corrected Charlotte. "It was soap."

"Still," said Jude, "it made people feel pretty sick." She wrote it down. "Kitchen mess. Soap in food. What else?"

"Mugging in the park," murmured Zibby.

"And the wallet getting stolen," said Jude, writing it all down. "There. Anything else?"

"Her headaches," Zibby said slowly. "I think you should add those, even though they're not just one incident. Because my mom has been having headaches and neck aches, really bad ones, a lot. And I think they started just after the bride's head fell off."

"Headaches could just come from stress, though," Jude pointed out. "Weddings are fun, but they're a lot of work to put together."

"Not to mention the stress of having Laura-Jane for your stepdaughter!" added Charlotte. "I get a headache just thinking about her — and I don't even have to live with her!"

"But I think my mom's headaches started after Laura-Jane pulled off the mother doll's head," remembered Zibby. "I'm sure there's a connection."

She took the Primrose doll out of her pocket and smoothed the brown braids. "Primrose? Are you with us?"

*Indeed I am.*

The voice, of course, was only in Zibby's head. "She's here," Zibby told the other girls, and propped the little doll carefully against a low branch. The girls linked hands.

"Can you add anything to Jude's list?" Zibby asked the ghost.

*There's Laura-Jane's unpleasant disposition,* the ghostly voice told them. *What about that?*

"But how could that be due to Miss Honeywell?" asked Charlotte. "That's just inborn nastiness."

Something was still bothering Zibby, niggling in the back of her mind. Something about the list that didn't quite fit. What was it?

*Laura-Jane is an unhappy child,* pronounced Primrose. *She needs —*

"She needs a good punch in the chops," said Charlotte, and Penny giggled.

*Interruption is a sign of poor breeding,* replied Primrose.

Charlotte blushed and Zibby tried not to smile. Charlotte of all the girls would hate to be accused of poor manners.

"But Laura-Jane is the one who played the horrible game with the dollhouse dolls," Jude explained to Primrose. "It was Laura-Jane who set all this in motion. Okay, I suppose she doesn't know what she's done — I

147

mean, how could she? But that she played such mean games at all is proof of her — of her *badness*."

Zibby nodded, remembering all the other frightening things that Miss Honeywell had done after she and her friends had played with the house — before they'd made the connection that the doll-play was coming true in a horribly altered fashion. The niggling sense of something not quite right grew stronger. She stared at the leaves overhead, thinking.

Then she knew. "Wait, Jude. Maybe we've got it wrong."

*Aha*, chirped Primrose. *Now you're using your head.*

"What do you mean?" asked Jude.

"I mean things haven't been happening the way Miss Honeywell makes things happen."

Charlotte had been shredding green leaves between her fingers. Now she tossed the fragments into the air. The girls watched the pieces drop onto the dirt. "What do you mean? It's just like what Miss Honeywell did before."

"But it isn't, Char," said Zibby slowly. "Not really." She tried to make clear to the other girls what had suddenly come clear in her own mind. It was Jude's list that made her think of it. The attacks and injuries made a frightening chronicle of someone's malevolence. Because the horrible things had started happening right after Laura-Jane played with the dollhouse, Zibby had connected them to Miss Honeywell. But the terrible things Miss Honeywell had done in the past were different from these.

"Don't you see?" she tried to explain. "Whatever bad things happened before, they happened after we'd played a similar game in the dollhouse. Remember, we played that my friend, Amy, came to visit. Then what really happened was that Amy and her dad got into an accident while trying to come visit us. Or remember those thieves. Or what about Jude's dad? That was awful. But you see? We played with the dolls first, and then the ghost was able to, you know, *pervert* the game in her own evil way — but based on what we had played first. But except for my mom's headaches that started after Laura-Jane pulled the doll's head off, the rest of the bad things have happened even though nobody has been playing with the dolls."

"But maybe Laura-Jane has been sneaking in to play with the dollhouse when you're not there to see her," said Penny.

"Or maybe Miss Honeywell has changed her method of attack," theorized Charlotte.

"Or maybe it's someone *else* doing it all," said Jude. "Someone who keeps getting away with a lot of vicious attacks because we keep thinking it has to be the work of the ghost!" She looked around at the little group. "But if not Miss Honeywell, then who?"

*Aha*, said Primrose Parson in Zibby's head. *Now you're thinking!*

A shiver pounced down Zibby's spine. It was frightening enough to think that the ghost of Miss Honeywell was responsible for the terrible things that had been happening to Nell. But what if it weren't the ghost? What if it weren't a ghost at all, but a real person? Some people — people who feared the supernatural above all things — might be comforted by the thought. But not Zibby. The thought of some unknown person trying to hurt her mom made the danger more real, and frightened Zibby more than ever.

"Well," she said forcefully. "I bet I know who it is, then. Those Ballantynes! The new caterers in town. I saw how that woman looked at my mom. She was green with jealousy. And that man!"

"Yeah," nodded Penny. "He was rude at the wedding reception. I didn't like him."

"And he's tall," said Zibby. "My mom said the attacker was taller than she is."

"And the Ballantynes were around on the day the whipped cream was tampered with," remembered Jude. "When we drove away, they were still looking inside the hall. They could easily have slipped inside . . . "

"It makes sense," agreed Charlotte. "If they can put Aunt Nell out of business, they can corner the market in Carroway and get everyone's business!"

"Well, how can we catch them?" asked Penny. "I mean, that's what we need to do now, isn't it? We can't just sit here talking about them — maybe this, maybe that. We need to watch them and wait for them to try something else, and then we go straight to the police."

The older girls looked at Penny with respect. "Spies!" said Jude. "Right, Penny, that's what we'll have to be." She pretended to twirl a mustache. "We'll track them to their lair."

Charlotte flipped back her long hair with a disdainful gesture. "It's not a game, Jude. I think we should just go straight to the police. I don't want to skulk around town like little kids playing spies."

"You can't just call the police without any evidence," Jude retorted.

Charlotte stood up. "Well, I won't make a fool of myself hiding under windows, peering inside and acting ridiculous. The police are already interested in knowing who might have a grudge against Aunt Nell. All I want to do is tell them how the Ballantynes were rude and seemed jealous. Then the police can decide to investigate or not." She ducked under the branches of the clubhouse. "I'm going home to call them now."

Zibby shrugged at Jude and Penny. Her cousin was known for her impatience.

"I don't think it's ridiculous to spy on them, do you?" asked Penny.

"I don't exactly feel like hiding in the bushes or anything," admitted Zibby. "But I do agree that the Ballantynes are the likeliest bad guys. It can't hurt for Charlotte to tell the police what we suspect."

Mrs. Jefferson called from the back door for Penny and Jude to come inside for lunch. Jude ducked under the branches. "Coming, Nana!" she called. She turned back to Zibby. "Want to eat with us?"

Zibby shook her head. "No thanks. I'd better get back and see how my mom's doing." She felt strongly protective of her mom. She didn't want Nell out of her sight for long.

"Okay," Jude said, "but after lunch we can ride our bikes to the Ballantynes' house."

"Just to look around," added Penny. "We don't have to peer into the windows if you don't want to."

"Fine." Zibby scooted out of the bower of branches and stood up. She flapped her hand in a wave. "See you later."

She set off back down the street to her house. Toward her on his bike came the now familiar figure of Todd, his blond hair sticking out from under his bike helmet. He was riding his mountain bike as if it were a unicycle, tipped back on one wheel. Astonishingly, he didn't look at all unsteady, but pedaled along with aplomb. *He really should be in the circus,* Zibby thought in admiration.

"Hi, Todd!" she called.

He braked to a stop. "Hello, Zibby."

"Were you just visiting Laura-Jane?" Zibby asked. This might be a good time to talk to him about Laura-Jane's attitude.

"No way!" he exclaimed. Then, when Zibby looked

at him in surprise, added with a smile: "I mean, I probably shouldn't go over until she's un-grounded, wouldn't you say?"

"I guess so," Zibby agreed. "But you could be a good influence on her, you know? I mean, she's in trouble because of the way she's acting — really hostile to my mom and running off without telling where she's going. . . . She really admires you, and so I was wondering whether —" her voice trailed off as he continued to stand there grinning down at her. "What?"

"You. You're a nice kid, you know? Wanting to help her. Sure, I'll try to be a good influence on her." He laughed. "I'll steer her away from a life of crime and evil!"

Zibby had to laugh back. He tipped his bike back up on one wheel again. "Well, I'm in a hurry — gotta go! I'll see you around!" he called, and she waved as he cycled expertly toward the park. For a second, as she watched, it seemed there was another rider in the distance — a rider on a bike, dressed in gray. Then she blinked, and there was only Todd again.

Zibby wondered briefly where he was going to in such a hurry. She wished he'd had time to stay and talk longer. It was a new experience for Zibby to feel it might be fun to hang out with a boy — fun to get to know him as someone special, maybe even as more than just a friend.

She wished she'd thought to tell him to be careful riding in the park. If the mugger weren't Hector Ballantyne out especially to attack Nell, then anyone could be at risk. She hated to think of Todd's smiling face coming under attack from an assailant. But Todd's gymnastic training had made him strong. He could beat weedy Hector to a pulp in no time.

Cheered at this thought, Zibby climbed the steps of the porch. Inside, the house was quiet. She found her mom and Ned with Brady in the backyard. They were sitting on the patio at the picnic table, shaded by a large yellow and blue umbrella. They were eating tuna salad and drinking lemonade.

"Hi," said Zibby. "How are you feeling, Mom?"

"I'm fine, honey. Now that the nosebleed has stopped and I've cleaned myself up, I only have the scratches to show for my adventure."

"Some adventure," muttered Ned.

"I'm going to be Nell's guard," Brady said eagerly. "I'm going to stay with her the whole day so nothing else can hurt her."

"You're a sweet little boy, Brady, you know that?" Nell hugged him. Zibby winced when she saw the Band-Aids on her mom's hands.

"Any lunch for me?" Zibby asked.

"Yes indeed," smiled Nell. "Go get yourself a plate from the kitchen, honey. And there's fruit salad in a bowl on the counter. Will you bring it out?"

"Sure." Zibby turned to go back into the house.

"Zibby, would you mind going up to Laura-Jane's room and asking her to come on out here for lunch?"

Ned added. "Just because she's grounded from going away from the house, there's no reason why she can't join us for meals."

"She's sulking," said Nell. "I don't think she'll want to eat lunch with us."

"Well, I want her to," he maintained, and Zibby went inside and headed up the stairs.

She knocked on Laura-Jane's door. There was no answer. She opened the door and saw that the room was empty. Then she heard the toilet flushing downstairs and knew Laura-Jane was in the bathroom. She sat down in Laura-Jane's armchair to wait, and reached back to adjust the cross-stitched pillow behind her.

Her fingers touched something hard. Something smooth and firm. She shifted in the chair and moved the pillow, drew out the object — and sucked in her breath sharply.

Nell's black leather wallet.

# Chapter 13

Zibby heard Laura-Jane's footsteps on the attic stairs through the roar of blood pounding in her head. She shoved the wallet back under the pillow just as Laura-Jane came into the room.

"What are you doing here, Zibby?" Laura-Jane asked sullenly.

"Your dad wants you to come down and eat lunch. They're out on the patio." She was surprised her voice came out sounding so normal while her mind raced along like a wild thing.

So it had been Laura-Jane all the time! The knowledge sickened her, but it made perfect sense. After all, it had never been a secret that Laura-Jane hated Nell. It was a short leap from inactively hating to actively trying to hurt someone. Laura-Jane was at the reception when the tires were slashed. Laura-Jane must somehow have wrecked the food for the catered party and spiked the whipped cream with soap powder, too — although,

156

hadn't she been up in her room when they'd left with the food in the van? When would she have had time to tamper with it?

*Nonetheless*, Zibby thought firmly, *the evidence was compelling*. And the wallet was the best proof of all. She flushed as she thought of her mom, wanting only to be helpful, going to the park to search for Ned's wayward children — and all the time one of those children was lurking in the bushes waiting to mug her! How dare Laura-Jane sneak up behind Nell and push her down? How dare she smash her face into the dirt and steal her wallet?

"I don't feel like eating lunch," Laura-Jane said in her whispery voice. Was it Zibby's imagination, or did that voice sound nervous?

Well Laura-Jane *should* be nervous. With a surge of anger, Zibby drew the wallet from behind the pillow and threw it on the bed.

"How dare you?" she asked flatly.

Laura-Jane sank onto her bed. Her face grew very pale and her dark eyes closed. "I didn't," she whispered.

"You did. And here's the proof."

"No." Laura-Jane opened her eyes. They blazed hotly. "I never meant for it to happen."

Zibby reached out and scooped up the wallet. She walked to the door. "My mom will be glad to get this back. Is the money still there? Or did you spend it?"

"I didn't — oh, Zibby, I was going to give it back to

her. I *was!*" The raspy voice was choked. The black eyes were pleading.

But Zibby was not moved. Her anger burned in her like a torch. It made her own eyes glitter and her skin feel tingly, as if an electric current blazed inside her. All her energy was focused in this room, toward this girl who was now her stepsister.

Everything was Laura-Jane's fault. There was no excuse for what Laura-Jane had done — none at all — and Zibby would show no mercy. "The police will be happy to see this wallet," she said grimly. "And to hear where I found it."

"Zibby, *please!*" begged Laura-Jane. "I *was* going to give it back. I really was! I never meant for your mom to get hurt —"

Zibby laughed coldly. It was a chilling sound and cooled the anger inside her. Now, as she listened to Laura-Jane rush on with her excuses, with her explanations of how she wasn't really to blame, Zibby felt only numb. She took no pleasure in turning Laura-Jane in to the police, in revealing to Ned and Nell how deep her hatred ran. She knew they would be badly shaken. But at last all the trouble and worries would stop. With Laura-Jane safely locked up wherever they locked cruel, delinquent kids away, family life could get back to normal, and Zibby's fears for Nell's safety would disappear.

Now Laura-Jane was hanging on Zibby's arm, digging her nails in hard, pleading with her in the same

158

whispery, expressionless voice not to tell Ned, not to tell the police. Zibby was surprised at how strong Laura-Jane's thin fingers felt. "Get off!" she yelled at Laura-Jane.

A voice calling up the stairs caused them both to freeze, staring at each other.

"What's going on up there?" It was Ned's voice, sounding somehow angry and weary at the same time. "Zibby? I asked you only to call Laura-Jane down for lunch. There's no need to have any sort of argument with her."

"Please don't say anything," Laura-Jane begged again. "Let me handle this my own way."

"I don't trust your 'own way,'" retorted Zibby, also in a whisper.

"I promise I'll give the wallet back. I promise. Just give me some time."

Zibby slipped the wallet into her own pocket. She didn't want to give in. Laura-Jane deserved no pity. But Ned's weary voice echoed in her head and she felt sorry that he would soon know he had a monster for a daughter. For Ned, she would give Laura-Jane the extra time. "Oh, all right," she said as the two of them moved out of the room and down the stairs to where Ned waited, his face dark with thunder. "You have till bedtime tonight. But I'm keeping this wallet till then. And if anything else happens to my mom . . ."

"It won't!" said Laura-Jane, pushing ahead of Zibby on the stairs.

They ate lunch in strained silence. Nell and Brady made light conversation for a few minutes, then grew quiet. Brady ran off to kick a soccer ball around in the yard. Ned glanced at his watch and said he had to get to the newspaper office. He hadn't been to work that day, due to the morning's unpleasant events. "I'll be home late," he told Nell as he kissed her. "Not till nine or so."

"That's fine," she told him. "The kids and I will be fine. Right, girls?" she smiled brightly at Zibby and Laura-Jane.

Both of them nodded. Then Ned looked hard at his daughter. "Laura-Jane, I expect perfect behavior from you. Is that clear?"

"Yes, Daddy," she whispered, her eyes downcast.

*She looks meek enough to fool anyone,* Zibby thought. *But not me!* She excused herself and went to call Jude. There would be no need, now, to spy on Hilda and Hector Ballantyne.

The Jeffersons' phone was busy. Zibby punched the buttons of Charlotte's number. Her cousin's line was busy, too. Probably Jude and Penny were talking to Charlotte. Probably they were wondering how best to track down the new caterers in town. Well, they were wasting their time. "The enemy is among us," Zibby murmured dramatically to herself as she started up the stairs to her room.

*Don't be so sure of that.*

160

"Oh, Primrose, I was just coming up to see you," said Zibby. She walked into her room and picked up the little doll from the bedside table. "The mystery of the murderous stepsister is solved. It was Laura-Jane!"

*Don't jump to conclusions, my girl. I know Miss Honeywell is lurking about. I can feel her presence in the house. She wants me to go in so she can keep me with her.* The voice in Zibby's head was emphatic.

"Well, that may be true," said Zibby. "But at least that's a separate problem from what's been happening to my mom. Miss Honeywell isn't the one who has been making trouble this time. I was wrong about that. That was all Laura-Jane's doing." Zibby narrowed her eyes. "She should be locked up. And when I go to the police, she will be!"

*I agree that Miss Honeywell deserves to be locked up,* replied Primrose. *But not in my dollhouse. We have to get her out and locked up elsewhere.*

"Oh, Primrose — I'm talking about Laura-Jane!" Zibby propped the little girl doll against the pillow and sat down on the bed. "Laura-Jane is the one who is going to end up in prison — or reform school. And she deserves it."

*But what if you're wrong?*

"Of course I'm not wrong! I found the wallet in her bedroom, hidden behind the cushion on her chair — the cushion my own gram made. It's polluted now. Everything Laura-Jane touches is polluted. She stinks."

Zibby stared at the dollhouse with a frown, despising Laura-Jane, wishing she'd never heard of the girl. If Ned didn't have a daughter, life would be much nicer.

*The child is unpleasant, I'll not deny it,* came Primrose's reply. *But I do happen to have some information that might well shed a new light on the situation.*

"What information?" Zibby reached for the little doll and held her up.

*I have excellent powers of observation,* replied the ghost smugly. *I shall solve this mystery for you.*

Zibby frowned at the doll. She hated having to humor the ghost. As far as she was concerned, the mystery was already solved.

*And I'll be happy to tell you what I saw — if you arrange compensation for my help.*

"We've already made you some more artwork — nice framed stamps," said Zibby. "They should be dry now. Look!" She carried the doll over to her desk, where the girls had left the little framed pictures.

*Very nice indeed,* said Primrose dismissively. *But I was thinking more along the lines of a beaded chandelier.*

"Primrose!"

*A deal is a deal,* retorted the ghost. *That is, if you want to add my important information to your knowledge of the case.*

Zibby sighed. "Primrose — this is blackmail."

*Not at all!* objected the little voice. *Blackmail would be if I threatened to tell your mother about the time you stuffed that liver dinner she'd made you right down the garbage disposal as soon as she left the room — unless you made me a chandelier immediately!*

"How did you know about that liver?" Zibby demanded. The incident with the liver had happened weeks ago when Nell, with unusual firmness, insisted that Zibby taste just one bite of the dinner. But when her mom had left the room for a few minutes, Zibby quickly disposed of the unappetizing looking slab of meat. She must have had the doll in her pocket at the time.

*It's not blackmail at all,* Primrose continued primly. *It is simply good business sense.*

"I'll see what I can do." Zibby decided there was no use arguing with Primrose. She was sick and tired of quarrels. "But first you need to give me one good reason why I shouldn't tell the police about Laura-Jane. Did you see something? Hear something?"

*One is innocent until proven guilty,* said Primrose. Her voice was serene.

"But I do have proof," snapped Zibby.

*Circumstantial evidence, that's all. You'll feel very foolish and do your sister a grave disservice if you act in haste.*

"I hate it when you go all preachy on me, Primrose," said Zibby. "And Laura-Jane is not my sister."

*Please to try to remember that though I have chosen to reside in this little girl doll, my spirit is old and wise, my dear. Now be a good child and make me my chandelier. It should be quite like the one in our dining room when I was a girl. Miss Honeywell always liked that chandelier, I recall. She liked fancy things like that, but had none of her own. Not that she deserved anything so fine . . .*

Zibby shook her head as if to dislodge the irritating voice of her own personal ghost. "All right, Primrose. All right, already!" She would call the other girls and tell them that if they could come over and make the chandelier right now, maybe they'd get this mystery cleared up by the end of the day.

# Chapter Fourteen

Half an hour later Zibby, Jude, and Penny stood by Zibby's bedroom window, looking out and waiting for Charlotte to arrive. Zibby had told her friends only that they had done the Ballantynes a terrible wrong by suspecting them of conniving to hurt Nell. "They might be jealous of her success," she said, "but they're not the guilty ones."

"Who is?" demanded Jude.

But Zibby just shook her head. "Let's wait for Charlotte. I'll tell you all together."

"Cool bike," whistled Penny as Charlotte swept into the driveway on her shiny, red, fifteen-speed mountain bike. "Maybe I should ask for a bike like that for my birthday instead of a dollhouse, what do you think, Jude?"

Jude shrugged, looking out the window. "I think that bike costs a lot more than the dollhouse you'll be getting, so I wouldn't waste any time hoping. There's no way."

"That's what I like about you, my dear niece. You're always so optimistic." Penny elbowed Jude out of the way so she could get a better view of Charlotte's bike.

Zibby also admired the bike, not that she would ever let her cousin know it. Not that Charlotte really needed such a big deal bike, anyway. But Charlotte liked to have the best of everything — and had parents who didn't mind indulging her. Fortunately Charlotte wasn't stuck up, despite the grown-up air she cultivated. Nor was she selfish.

"I'm going to ask her to let me ride it," Penny declared.

"Fine," said Zibby. "But not now. Now we've got to get busy making a chandelier. Jude, you're the architect. How do we start?"

Jude laughed. "*You're* the carpenter! It's not like a building design, you know. I don't have the slightest idea. I thought you would."

"Well, maybe we can just somehow wind the beads around some wire and hang it from the ceiling."

*And it must work!* came Primrose's reedy voice in Zibby's head. *The chandelier needs candles or lightbulbs. You'll have to wire it for electricity.*

Zibby sighed. "Primrose says she wants the chandelier to really work."

Jude shook her head. "I don't know how to do that. It's going to be hard enough just figuring out how to make a chandelier!"

"Remember what we said about compromise," Zibby reminded Primrose.

*But I want it to sparkle!* wailed the ghostly voice.

"She wants it to sparkle," Zibby reported dourly.

Jude spoke soothingly, "Listen, Primrose. With the light shining on it from Zibby's lamp, it will still sparkle beautifully even without electricity."

They heard Charlotte's feet on the stairs. They all turned to greet her when she entered the room.

"Boy," Charlotte said, dramatically flipping her long blonde hair over her shoulders. "It's grim around here. First of all I encountered Laura-Jane, sitting on the porch swing like some kind of palace guard. She gave me a totally evil look when I went inside. I was afraid she'd stick a bayonet in me if I didn't know the password."

"What was the password?" Penny asked eagerly.

Charlotte gave her a withering look. "And then I found Aunt Nell just sitting in the kitchen with her head in her hands. Not the way a new bride should look at all. It's really sad. And Brady —"

"Never mind, Char." Zibby cut her off. "Everything will change around here once we get Laura-Jane packed off to reform school or wherever it is that thieves and muggers and food poisoners go when they're only ten years old."

"What do you mean? I know she's bad, but — reform school might be a bit much."

"I don't think so," said Zibby, and then she told the other girls about the wallet she'd found hidden under the cushion on Laura-Jane's chair.

"No way!" squealed Penny.

Jude looked stunned. "You mean she's been responsible for everything?"

Zibby nodded. "I think so — though Primrose is holding out on something she says is very important. I can't think what it is, so I promised her we'd make her the stupid chandelier in exchange for the information."

Charlotte pressed her lips together. "Well, Laura-Jane isn't nearly as frightening to me as Miss Honeywell is. She's a lot easier to catch, for one thing. Have you told Ned yet? He's going to freak out."

"I haven't told anyone yet," Zibby said. "And I haven't even given my mom back the wallet — because Laura-Jane begged me not to. She says she was planning to do it herself. And Primrose insists I shouldn't turn Laura-Jane into the police until I hear this big news."

"Well, if it's about Laura-Jane, I guess we'd better hear it," said Jude. "But let's get started. We're wasting time."

"And who knows whether Laura-Jane will be here when we finish," muttered Zibby. "That's the problem with my promise to wait till tonight to tell people about her. She might run away or something. And I'm not sure she'd be easier to catch than Miss Honeywell."

Penny turned to Charlotte. "So, did you bring the earrings?"

The dangly earrings that Charlotte pulled out of the pocket of her shorts were not really as valuable as they looked. But they certainly looked like something no eleven-year-old girl should be toting around town. *They look* thought Zibby, as Charlotte displayed the earrings on Zibby's bed, *like something a queen would wear.*

Aunt Linnea had given the pair to Charlotte when she'd cleaned out her jewel box. The earrings were only costume jewelry, she told her daughter, made of glass instead of real diamonds. Now the girls leaned over the twin earrings, admiring the way the light glinted on the cut surfaces of glass.

"They sure look like diamonds," said Penny admiringly. "Look how they glitter!"

"Well," said Jude practically. "You've heard the saying 'all that glitters isn't gold,' haven't you! And in this case, what's glittering isn't diamonds either. Just glass — and our ticket to hearing whatever big news Primrose Parson promises to tell us."

"So let's get busy," Charlotte said, and picked up the scissors from Zibby's desk. "I guess we'll have to cut the earring wire into shorter lengths and bend them somehow to make a chandelier shape."

"It's such a shame," mourned Penny.

"I'll get my mom's sewing box," Zibby said resolutely. "We'll probably need thread."

"Don't start yet," said Jude, examining the pair. She grabbed a piece of notepaper off Zibby's desk and sketched a rough plan of how they might fashion a chandelier out of the earrings. "It's better to make a diagram first so we know what we want to do."

Then they set to work. Zibby, who preferred carpentry work (with *large* pieces of wood), found her fingers cramping and her temper fraying very quickly. Penny had problems, too — with knotted thread and pricked thumbs. Charlotte and Jude worked competently, though largely in silence. Zibby was thinking about Laura-Jane's violence against Nell, and suspected the other girls were, too.

Finally the chandelier was finished. "There!" exulted Penny as she held up the finished product. The two earrings had been painstakingly reshaped and connected with white cotton thread, and now glittered in the late afternoon sunlight streaming through Zibby's windows.

"It looks great!" approved Charlotte. "Primrose will love it."

"She'd better love it," said Zibby. "Because a bargain is a bargain. Primrose!" She picked up the little doll. "Come on, then, Primrose. You've got your chandelier — now let's hear your big news."

*I like it.* The ghostly voice whispered through Zibby's mind. *It is lovely. I would like you to hang it in the dining room. Or perhaps the parlor. Or perhaps —*

"I'll hang it wherever you want it, but only after you tell us your piece of information."

*Young girls*, sighed Primrose, the sound like a mournful whistle in Zibby's head. *Young girls are often hasty. They jump to conclusions. But old souls like me — we know not to make rash judgments. We keep our own counsel and take action only when necessary. We sit and wait and watch what goes on.*

Zibby bit her lip to keep back the sharp retort. She reached for Jude's hand so her friend could hear the ghost as well. Charlotte and Penny joined hands with Jude and Zibby, and the circle of girls stood ringed around the tiny chandelier that lay glittering on the green carpet. "Just get on with it, Primrose," ordered Zibby. "Cut the lecture."

*We sit and wait and watch*, repeated Primrose's voice serenely, but this time they all heard it. *And soon enough we understand.*

"What did you see while you watched and waited?" asked Zibby impatiently. "What?"

*Your sister came into this room this morning while you were out*, replied the ghost. *And she was not alone. She and her friend closed the door and spoke in whispers. I did not hear all that was said. But she was crying. And her friend was angry.*

"She's not my sister —" began Zibby, but Jude interrupted.

"Her friend? Who was her friend?"

*It was the boy. The boy with blond hair who moves like a panther.*

171

"Todd?" said Zibby. "But when I talked to him, he said he hadn't seen Laura-Jane today."

"So maybe he lied," said Charlotte. "Go on, Primrose. What does that have to do with all the horrible things Laura-Jane's done to Nell?

*Perhaps nothing,* replied Primrose softly. *But perhaps everything. The boy, you see, threw something at her in his anger.*

"Something?" repeated Zibby. She looked over at Jude and their eyes locked. What would the ghost reveal?

*A wallet,* said Primrose triumphantly. *He pulled a wallet from his pocket and threw it straight at her. It would have hit her in the face, but she caught it in time. She ran out of the room with it. And the boy stayed in here, looking around. He poked around in your desk. I didn't like that. Young people today have no sense of propriety. When he started opening your dresser drawers, I stopped him.*

"Stopped him?" asked Zibby. She knew she sounded stupid, just repeating what Primrose said. But her thoughts were muddled and she was still trying to take in what the ghost was telling her. How could *Todd* have Nell's wallet?

*Stopped him in his unmannerly tracks,* said Primrose with satisfaction. *The little girl doll was sitting on your dresser, and I made her move, made her wave at him. Just a bit — but enough to scare that big handsome boy right out of the room!*

Zibby dropped her friends' hands and hugged herself. She felt suddenly chilled despite the warmth of the summer afternoon. *Todd* couldn't have anything to

172

do with this. "Not Todd," she mumbled. "I won't believe it."

"I think the next thing we have to do," Jude said decisively, "is talk to Laura-Jane."

The four girls moved to the door with one accord. *Wait!* clamored Primrose's imperious voice in Zibby's head. *What about my chandelier! I want you to hang it in the parlor — and I want you to do it right now!*

# Chapter 15

Zibby ignored the ghost's insistent plea. She led the way up to Laura-Jane's attic bedroom. Laura-Jane was standing in the doorway when they reached the top of the stairs. It was almost as though she were waiting for them, thought Zibby.

"What were you and Todd doing in my bedroom?" Zibby demanded without preamble.

Laura-Jane groaned. "Who told you about that?"

"And how did Todd get hold of Aunt Nell's wallet?" asked Charlotte loudly.

Laura-Jane seemed to deflate like a leaky balloon. She sagged against the door frame. "Keep your voices down and I'll tell you." She frowned. "At least, I'll tell *you*, Zibby." She looked at the other girls distastefully.

"You'll tell all of us," Zibby retorted.

"Why?"

"Because they're worried about my mom. They care about her. Not like *some* people I could mention."

"Yeah!" cried Penny.

Jude was looking past Laura-Jane into the cozy bedroom. "Can we sit in here, maybe?"

Laura-Jane hesitated, then stepped aside so the others could enter her bedroom. Jude sat in the chair where Zibby had found the wallet. Zibby sat at Laura-Jane's desk. Charlotte sank onto Laura-Jane's bed. Penny sat cross-legged on the floor by the pink doll-house. There was not much room left for Laura-Jane in the small room. She remained standing by the door rather than sit next to Charlotte on the bed.

"How did you know Todd was here?" asked Laura-Jane again as soon as the girls had settled.

Zibby looked at Jude. If she answered Laura-Jane's question honestly, she would have to tell her stepsister about Primrose. Jude shook her head ever so slightly. So Zibby just shrugged. "Someone told me."

"Someone? Who?"

"Forget who. Why was Todd here?" pressed Jude.

"I didn't know he was coming over." Laura-Jane said defensively. "Really! I knew Dad would be furious. But Todd came by and said he had to talk to me urgently — that's what he said, *urgently*. And so I was going to bring him upstairs to my room so we could talk privately. On the way up the stairs, we heard Brady up in his room — so I pulled him into Zibby's room instead. That's all."

"That's not all," said Zibby harshly.

"There's the little problem of what he had with him . . ." said Charlotte.

"The wallet," added Penny helpfully.

"I was as shocked as you are!" Laura-Jane cried suddenly. "I didn't know a thing about it! I swear! He seemed so proud of himself, too. He tossed me the wallet and said, 'I did it!' and when I said I couldn't believe it, he just laughed. He said he knew it was what I'd wanted —"

"What? That he should mug Zibby's mom?" Jude shook her head, black braids snapping around her face.

"Of course I didn't want that," cried Laura-Jane.

"Didn't you?" asked Charlotte caustically. "We've heard how you played such a horrible game with the dollhouse dolls. Maybe you did want to hurt Aunt Nell. Maybe you wanted to *kill* her!"

"No!" Laura-Jane covered her face with her hands. "I was just upset about the wedding. I was so unhappy. And there wasn't anybody I could talk to about it. Everybody seemed to think it was so wonderful that they were getting married. Even my own *mom* said it was nice that he found someone who could make him happy!" Her voice trembled at the thought of this betrayal. She lowered her hands and peered at them. Her whisper rasped through the room like the sound of tearing paper. "Dad was so wrapped up in Nell, he had no time for me and Brady anymore. Oh, I know he did things with us, but his heart wasn't with us the way it had been before. It was like they were riding along in their own little private bubble of happiness — with no room for anyone else. And then I met Todd . . . and he was sweet. And easy to talk to — just like an older brother would be. Or a dad who had time for me . . . "

Laura-Jane fell silent. Zibby stared at her, confused feelings of sympathy mixing with the fury in her gut. She pushed the sympathy away. Laura-Jane wasn't worth it.

"So you told him how ticked off you were about your dad and Zibby's mom," Jude said encouragingly after Laura-Jane showed no sign of continuing her story.

Laura-Jane nodded slowly, slumping against the closed door of her room. "I said I wished someone would prick their little bubble. And Todd smiled and said he had an idea how we could make some real trouble for them."

"I don't believe that!" Zibby burst out. She had been toying with a pen at Laura-Jane's desk and now threw it down angrily. "Todd's not like that! I think you're just trying to blame it on him —"

"Maybe Todd's angry at mothers who go away," Penny said softly. "You told us his own mother went off to the circus, Zibby. He can't get at her to hurt her, so maybe he saw a chance with *your* mom. A sort of substitute."

Zibby looked at her friend in surprise. Penny's lightheartedness often made the others forget how clear-sighted she could be. But Jude was frowning.

"*My* mom has gone away," she reminded the others. "She's working in Africa. But I don't feel like getting even with her for it!"

"But you know your mom is coming back," Charlotte said, defending Penny's theory. "And she writes to you and phones you. Todd's mom just went off. Maybe he never hears from her or anything."

"He doesn't," Laura-Jane said eagerly. She left the door and came to perch on the bed next to Charlotte. "She even forgot to send a card for his birthday this year. His sixteenth birthday — and his mom didn't even remember."

"Well, that's sad," agreed Jude. "But it's no excuse to go around hurting other people's mothers! And you let him! That's really terrible, Laura-Jane."

"I know," Laura-Jane murmured. "But it didn't start out being so bad. I mean, it started more as a prank. When Todd suggested puncturing the tires of the van during the wedding reception, I thought it was a good idea. I knew Dad and Nell wouldn't be hurt, and it would just, well, you know, let a little air out of their bubble, I guess."

"It was mean of you." Penny frowned.

"They could have been killed," said Charlotte. "Sometimes when a car gets a flat tire, it's hard to control. And they had *four* flats."

"I didn't think of that." Laura-Jane leaned over so that her black hair swung forward like a curtain, hiding her face. "And I didn't think that messing up the trays of food in the kitchen would do much harm, either. It was my idea to, well, make some trouble for Nell. Because I was so mad at her and Dad. I was just going to tip one of the trays onto the floor or something. Or spill some milk onto her little tarts — I don't know. But then Todd said he'd plan it for me — as a friend. He said I wouldn't even have to be around while he did it. But he went crazy or something. I had no idea he'd totally trash the whole room and wreck everything — and break all the china and stuff. I had no idea the police would be called in! That was when I felt really sick about what we'd done."

Zibby had been sitting silently, her hands clenched into tight fists. The refrain of *not Todd, not Todd* kept beating in her heart. But it *had* been Todd. Todd and Laura-Jane. Now she thumped her fists hard on Laura-Jane's desk and jumped up. Her eyes blazed with anger. "Okay, great! Just a few little pranks, huh? Then how do you explain the rest? Food poisoning? Mugging? Stealing a wallet? That's doing a bit more than just letting air out of the balloon, don't you think? That's popping the balloon and ripping it to shreds and —"

"But I didn't do those other things, Zibby," Laura-Jane interrupted in a strangled voice. "I swear I didn't! After he wrecked the kitchen and all the party food, I told him that was enough, *more* than enough. I told him he was going too far, and that we'd made enough trouble. He laughed at me! He told me today that he stole some of the soap powder from the Pizza Den where he works and dumped it in the whipped cream. He said he'd seen Nell in the park and decided to attack her. He said he was really enjoying all of this, and that Nell deserved it, and that this was just the beginning!"

"And you didn't try to stop him," said Jude.

Laura-Jane slumped. "I don't know how," she whispered. "He seemed so wonderful to me at first — but he scares me now."

Zibby drew in her breath sharply. She, too, had found Todd wonderful. The truth hurt. It hurt terribly.

Jude, after a quick sidelong glance at her friend, sized up the situation and spoke briskly. "Well, it's a shame. He did seem nice. But now we know."

"Right," said Charlotte. "And I think the police had better see this wallet right away so they can look for fingerprints on it. We should have thought of that before and not handled it so much. Maybe Todd's prints are still clear."

"We have to tell them they can stop suspecting the Ballantynes," added Penny.

Laura-Jane looked confused, so Penny explained about the rival caterers. Zibby sat silent and numb, thinking about all Laura-Jane had told them. She felt queasy, as if she were sitting in a small boat, bobbing in a rough sea. Laura-Jane's confession about her own part in the mean tricks and her revelations about Todd Parkfield certainly explained most of the mystery of all that had been going wrong. And she was relieved to know that the violence had had a human face behind it, and not a ghostly one. So why didn't she feel relieved, now that the mystery was solved?

Jude stood up. "Okay, Zibby?"

Zibby looked at her friend and nodded slowly.

Nell's voice calling up the stairs made them all start.

Zibby left the room and looked down the flight of attic steps at her mom and her cousin, Owen, who stood in the hallway below. "We're all up here," she said.

"All of you?" asked Nell. "Laura-Jane, too?"

"Yup."

Nell looked pleased. *She won't look very pleased when she learns what we've been talking about up here,* Zibby thought sadly.

"Owen's here to get Charlotte," Nell said. "Uncle David's brother and family are arriving this afternoon from Philadelphia, and Aunt Linnea wants her home."

"Mom says she has to clean her pigsty of a room before the cousins get here," Owen informed her.

"Okay," said Zibby. "We'll be down in a sec."

But Owen was on his way up. "Cool," he said appreciatively, looking around the attic. He was tall, like Charlotte, with the same blond hair, though his was cut very short. His blue eyes took everything in. "Last time I came up here it was just storage space full of cobwebs." He peeked into Brady's room, then stepped into Laura-Jane's. "Nice room," he said.

"What are you doing here, Owen?" Charlotte demanded.

"Time to go home, kiddo. I was at Jim's house and Mom phoned to say I should come home and get you on my way. Uncle Paul will be here soon and —"

Charlotte sighed. "I know, I know. My pigsty of a

181

room." She looked around at Laura-Jane's room. "How do you keep it so neat?" she asked.

Laura-Jane just shrugged. She didn't look at Charlotte's big brother, but stood looking out the window.

"Probably because she's not in it very often," said Zibby waspishly. "She's out with Todd Parkfield — scheming." She was pleased to see her stepsister flinch.

Owen frowned. "Todd Parkfield? You still hanging out with him?" He shook his head. "I'd watch out, if I were you. He can seem really friendly, but it's just a coverup for a pretty nasty personality. He didn't used to be so bad, but a couple of years ago he seemed to turn, I don't know, somehow *sour*."

"When his mom ditched him, probably," said Laura-Jane in an expressionless voice.

Owen snorted. "Maybe. But I'm not sure that's a very good excuse. Anyway, Parkfield could have a lot going for him — he's a super gymnast, best in the whole school. But rumor has it he's a troublemaker." He shook his head. "That kid is heading for jail one day — that's what I bet."

The girls looked at each other. "I bet it, too," Zibby muttered under her breath. "And sooner than you think."

# Chapter 16

That evening, after Jude and Penny had gone home, Zibby sat with her mom and stepfamily at the dining room table. Now that there were more people in the house, they tended to eat supper in the formal dining room under the twin chandeliers. When Zibby and her mom had lived alone, they ate at the little kitchen table. It seemed strange to Zibby that there should be a man sitting across the big rectangular table from her mom — in her dad's old chair. And stranger, still, to have two extra chairs at the table. Brady sat next to Zibby and Laura-Jane sat across from them. Brady ate quickly, eager to run back outside to play with the children across the street. Laura-Jane picked at her food, eyes downcast.

They finished their lasagna and salad, and Ned cleared the plates while Nell brought in a homemade raspberry sorbet. Brady eyed it suspiciously and asked if he could have a Popsicle to take outside instead.

Laura-Jane shook her head when Nell offered her a bowl, then changed her mind and glanced up with a tentative smile. "Yes, please," she whispered.

*Trying to get on Mom's good side,* Zibby thought sourly.

When Brady had raced out of the house to join the other children in a backyard game of tag, Nell cleared her throat. "I had a phone call while I was making supper," she announced. "From Hilda Ballantyne."

Laura-Jane looked up from her sorbet, eyes wary.

"She said the police had come around to her house to ask them about the mugging."

"Was she ticked off??" asked Zibby. "*I'd* be mad if the police accused me unfairly of mugging people!" She glanced pointedly over at Laura-Jane.

"We don't know if the accusation is unfair yet," Ned pointed out, and Zibby felt uncomfortable. What would he do when he heard Laura-Jane's confession?

"And I'm sure the police were polite," Nell added. "They probably just asked where the Ballantynes were today during the time I was in the park. Hilda didn't sound mad at all. She seemed very concerned about me, and said how sorry she was to hear what had happened. She told me about how she'd once had her purse snatched in the Paris Metro — and then she offered to make some meals for me to freeze so I wouldn't have to cook for a few days."

"I suppose it could have been her husband, acting alone," Ned mused. "The Ballantynes really are the most likely suspects, seeing how jealous and rude they've been to you. I'm not sure I'd trust Hilda Ballantyne's cooking!"

"Well, Hilda actually seemed nice this time. Someone who might be interesting to know — if the rivalry weren't there." Nell sighed.

"I bet the Ballantynes are innocent," said Zibby. "I bet it'll turn out to be the way it is in crime films — that the most likely suspect isn't the one who did it at all. It'll turn out to be the last person anybody suspected." *The cutest guy with the best smile in the world,* she thought, then pushed the last clouds of attraction resolutely from her mind.

"That's a frightening thought, isn't it?" said Nell. "I'd rather have my bad guys clearly labeled. And my friends, too. It's enough to give me nightmares — the idea that people aren't always what they seem to be."

Laura-Jane pushed back her bowl abruptly and stood up. "Excuse me," she mumbled, then left the room. They heard her footsteps on the stairs.

Ned and Nell exchanged a quizzical look. Zibby, watching, found her eyes drawn upward to the chandelier hanging from the ceiling above Nell's chair. Was it her imagination, or had it moved? The cut-glass baubles trembled slightly, clicking together. But there was no breeze from the open window.

Zibby cleared the table. Then while Nell and Ned sat outside on the porch swing watching Brady play ball in the front yard, she washed the supper dishes. She was just hanging up the damp dish towel when

Primrose's little voice rang inside her head: *What about my chandelier?*

"So that was you, wasn't it, moving the chandelier?" muttered Zibby. With so much turmoil, the dollhouse furnishings were the last thing on her mind. And yet she had promised Primrose. And Primrose *had* led them to Todd.

*It was that nice-looking blond boy, wasn't it?* said Primrose sadly. *And he looked like such a promising young man, too. Now with Miss Honeywell, you knew what to expect. She looked like a wrinkled, mean old prune on the outside — and was on the inside, too. And still is, even as a ghost.*

"But Miss Honeywell hasn't had anything to do with what's been happening to my mom," Zibby said as she climbed the stairs to her room. "It was Laura-Jane and Todd. Just because Miss Honeywell looks like a prune —"

She broke off and stared at her closed bedroom door. Hadn't she left it open?

Zibby put out her hand and turned the bedroom doorknob. The door swung open. Zibby held her breath, half expecting to see Miss Honeywell's gray-skirted figure and stern prune face. Instead she saw Laura-Jane, crouched down by the dollhouse. She was moving the dolls around and murmuring to herself, and didn't look up even when Zibby crossed the carpet and stood directly behind her.

*My chandelier!* nagged Primrose. But Zibby stood transfixed, watching Laura-Jane.

Laura-Jane held one of the little girl dolls and the mother doll. She moved them into the living room and sat them on the couch. "'I have to tell you everything,'" she said softly, tipping the girl doll to indicate who was speaking.

"'I don't want to hear anything you have to say, you horrible brat,'" the mother doll replied.

"'Please. It's about the bad things that have been happening to you. You know?'"

"'Do I know!'" snapped the mother doll.

"'Well, it wasn't the Ballantynes doing those things. It was Todd. And me.'"

"'I'm not surprised, you vicious thing, you!'" shrieked the mother doll. "'I always knew you were no good, and now your dad and I will send you away to reform school where you belong. It will be much nicer around here without you. We never liked you anyway.'"

Zibby opened her mouth to object, but before she could speak, Laura-Jane dropped the dolls and rubbed her eyes. Her shoulders heaved as though she were crying, but she made no sound. After a second, she picked up the dolls again.

"Okay," she whispered. "Let's try that again." She moved the dolls into the kitchen and sat them at the table. "'Nell?'" she made the little girl doll say. "'I have a terrible confession to make.'" Then Laura-Jane shook her head. "No, let's see. 'Nell? I have to tell you something. It's terrible, and I know you'll hate me more than you probably already do, and I can't blame you. But

187

please, please don't let the police arrest me and send me away to reform school!'"

Laura-Jane tipped the mother doll. "'Reform school is too good for you, you evil girl.'"

"'Please — '" cried the little girl doll.

"'Only death is good enough for you!'" shouted the mother doll, advancing on the little girl doll with arms outstretched. Zibby, crouching behind Laura-Jane to watch this drama, gasped as Laura-Jane made the mother doll grab the girl doll and throw her to the floor.

"No, wait, don't play that!" Zibby cried, shocked, as Laura-Jane made the mother doll jump up and down on the little girl doll. "Don't play that you die! You don't understand —"

Laura-Jane pushed Zibby away, then reached for the father doll. She walked him into the kitchen. "'Oh, my, why is Laura-Jane on the floor, dear?'" she made him ask in a hearty voice.

"'She's dead.'"

"'Oh, dear,'" said the father doll. "'But never mind. It's no less than she deserves —'"

Now Zibby reached out and snatched the dolls away. "You idiot! You can't play games like that with these dolls. You don't understand about Miss Honeywell!" She stopped, staring at Laura-Jane in fear. "You don't understand that what you play can happen in real life. Miss Honeywell can make what you play with the dolls come true!" But it wasn't Miss Honeywell who had been making all the bad things happen in real life, she thought in confusion. It was Todd.

Laura-Jane shrugged. "I'm just practicing. Getting up my courage to face your mom. What do you mean about Miss Honeywell? Who is that?" She frowned at Zibby. "I may be headed for reform school, but you're going to end up on a locked mental ward." She turned away and busied herself with tidying up the dollhouse rooms.

*It* had *been Todd,* Zibby told herself. So why was she still afraid of Miss Honeywell? *Because Primrose can't get into the house,* she thought. *And Mom still gets terrible headaches. And the bride doll's head fell off when Laura-Jane and Todd weren't even in the room*

Zibby knew the only way to stop Laura-Jane from playing any more dangerous games with the dollhouse dolls would be to tell her about the ghosts. And she knew she should check with the other club members before divulging such a secret. But there wasn't time. Laura-Jane had to play some other version of her game, quickly.

"Please listen to me even if you think I'm crazy," Zibby implored her stepsister now. "I know this sounds hard to believe. But I can prove it to you. My dollhouse is haunted. It's got two ghosts who both want to live in it. Most of the time Primrose Parson lives in it. She's okay — she's pretty nice most of the time. But Miss Honeywell, who used to be Primrose's governess, is bad news. She's cruel. And she's the one who is in the dollhouse now." Zibby glanced over to see how Laura-Jane was taking this information.

Laura-Jane was regarding her stonily.

"It was hard for me to believe at first, too," Zibby said earnestly. "But it's true — and you can ask Jude and Penny and Charlotte, too, They'll tell you!"

"Look, Zibby, let's just forget it, okay?" Laura-Jane's voice sounded tired. She looked tired, too. Haggard and thin, with her black hair hanging in two lank ponytails. "I don't know what you're trying to pull over on me, but I don't have time for it. I've got to go down now and tell my dad and your mom about Todd — and about my part in all this. That's hard enough for me. I don't want to hear silly ghost stories, too."

"You can't go yet, Laura-Jane! Not until you've played something else with the dolls, to cancel out what you just played. And fast. Miss Honeywell is mean. Worse than Todd, even. She likes to take whatever kids play with the dolls and make it come true in some nastier way." Quickly Zibby chronicled all the things Miss Honeywell had done in the past after someone had played with the dollhouse. "And then you played that the mother doll died — and all those bad things started happening to my mom in real life."

"But you know now that those things happened because of Todd — and me, too. It couldn't have been Miss Honey-whoever. Not that I believe in ghosts, anyway."

"Listen," Zibby pressed urgently. "I know now that

190

most of the bad stuff was Todd's fault. But there are still some things that have happened that Todd couldn't have done. The headaches. The bride doll. Unless *you* were the one who somehow crept in and beheaded the bride doll on the wedding cake?"

At Laura-Jane's uncomprehending look, Zibby told her about what had happened at the wedding reception. "And the blinding headaches, too. My mom still gets them. But she never got them before you pulled the mother doll's head off."

Laura-Jane frowned. "So if I play that your mom is so mad when I tell her about me and Todd that she kills me, you think Miss Honeywell will make her *really* kill me?" For the first time Laura-Jane's voice cracked. "Well, I'm surprised you don't think it's what I deserve!"

"Of course you don't deserve to die," Zibby answered brusquely. "You know that as well as I do. And my mom isn't the killer type. But you can never be sure how Miss Honeywell will manipulate things once you've given her a scenario to work with. She might have you die by falling out a window or something. Come on now, quick! Let's get busy playing another version of how you tell my mom what you've done. Before Miss Honeywell gets busy instead."

"Oh, Zibby," sighed Laura-Jane. "I don't believe in ghosts."

Zibby was feeling desperate. Miss Honeywell might be up to her malevolent tricks even now. Too bad the ghosts weren't the white-sheeted characters from Halloween movies. Something Laura-Jane could see for herself. But these real ghosts were strange shivery presences, felt in dark rooms and appearing in dreams. You couldn't see them. They were little scratching noises, or voices inside your head . . .

Voices!

Zibby grinned in sudden relief. Now she knew how to prove to Laura-Jane that there were, too, such things as ghosts. "Primrose?" she called. "Primrose, I need you!"

Laura-Jane headed for the bedroom door. "I'm out of here."

"No, wait!" Zibby grabbed Laura-Jane's hand and held on tightly when her stepsister tried to pull away. "Primrose, you said you would help me. We made a bargain!"

*Indeed we did,* came Primrose's disgruntled voice. *And I am still waiting.*

Laura-Jane screamed. She wrenched her hand out of Zibby's. "What was that?" she whispered, wild-eyed. "Who said that about — about *waiting?*"

"That was Primrose Parson, I told you, she's one of the ghosts. She speaks to me inside my head, but if you're touching me you can hear her, too." Zibby stood up and closed her bedroom door, leaning against it to keep Laura-Jane from running out of the room. "Listen. She'll tell you about Miss Honeywell."

Laura-Jane looked queasy. Zibby reached for her hand again. "Primrose won't hurt you. Just listen to her." Zibby cleared her throat. "Primrose? I promise I will install your chandelier tonight — this very night — if you will convince Laura-Jane that she has to play something else in the dollhouse to cancel out the last game she played. Okay?"

*Promise?*

"Yes! Now tell Laura-Jane about Miss Honeywell!"

"It must be ventriloquism or something," Laura-Jane whispered to Zibby. "I've read about that, about people who can throw their voices. You could go into the circus with Todd —"

"I keep telling you! It's Primrose." She held tightly to Laura-Jane's thin fingers.

*Indeed it is,* came Primrose's flutey voice. *A rather despondent ghost, I'm afraid. And I'm still waiting for my chandelier and my artwork. The girls promised me days and days ago, but have not kept their word. In my day, one could expect better standards.*

Laura-Jane stood rigidly next to Zibby. But at least she was no longer trying to pull away. "About Miss Honeywell," prompted Zibby.

*Miss Honeywell is an evil old crone.*

Laura-Jane pulled away from Zibby. "All right," she gasped. "I believe you! I believe you. But I don't want to hear anymore. I don't want to hear — that voice. Let's play whatever it is you want to play — and then I'm getting out of here."

*At last!* thought Zibby, heading back over to the

dollhouse. She reflected ruefully to herself that honesty really *was* the best policy, just as her mom had always said.

"Let's do it," Laura-Jane said tensely, kneeling on the floor in front of the dollhouse.

Zibby picked up the mother doll and handed Laura-Jane the girl doll. "I'll be my mom. You be yourself." She walked the Nell doll up the stairs. "'Yes, Laura-Jane? What did you want to see me about?'" she asked sweetly.

"'I need to tell you what I've done,'" said Laura-Jane, tipping the girl doll as she spoke.

"'Oh, dear,'" said the mother doll. "'What could it be?'"

"'It's all my fault — mine and Todd's. We let the air out of your tires for a mean joke — and then he got really excited and thought up the rest. I agreed to go along, but I didn't know he'd be so — so violent. I didn't know he was going to put soap in the food, or mug you in the park. I really, truly didn't, but I know you'll never forgive me and —'"

"'Of course I will,'" the mother doll cut in soothingly. "'I know you were just upset about the wedding.'" Zibby moved the mother doll forward and tipped it to kiss the little girl doll. "'There! Now we'll just forget all the unpleasant things that have happened and try to be a happy family. Okay? Now everything will be fine.'" Zibby laid the doll down on the couch. "The end."

Laura-Jane released the girl doll and left it on the

parlor floor. "We can't be a happy family. Not after everything that's happened. You don't want me in your family anyway."

"I didn't," Zibby said honestly. "But, oh, I don't know. It'll take some getting used to. For both of us." She wished she knew the right thing to say, the thing that would erase the terrible gloom from Laura-Jane's face and raise her voice up from the raspy whisper. "But legally now we're sisters. So maybe we could try to act like it."

Laura-Jane's dark hair swung forward and Zibby couldn't see her face. But she could hear her voice, and it was soft and sad. "I'll go down now and tell them in real life," Laura-Jane said. She reached out and smoothed the little girl doll's dress. "Then I'll call the police and tell them, too. And Zibby?" Now Laura-Jane looked up and Zibby saw that her eyes, for the first time, were full of tears.

"What?"

Laura-Jane reached out and touched Zibby's arm. "Thanks . . . "

And because they were touching, they both heard Primrose Parson's peevish voice: *Don't forget about my chandelier!*

# Chapter 17

Zibby hesitated. "I guess I'd better hang her stupid chandelier," she said. "Or we'll have no peace." *Not that there's ever much peace around here anyway*, she reflected wryly. Not since she'd bought the dollhouse, anyway.

"But I want you to come down with me," murmured Laura-Jane. "I want you to be there."

"All right. Just wait a minute." Zibby went to her desk and picked up the little chandelier and her plastic bottle of craft glue. She squeezed glue onto the little cardboard circle from which the chandelier hung, then walked over to the dollhouse. Laura-Jane watched from the doorway.

"Which room have you decided on in the end, Primrose?" asked Zibby. "The parlor or the dining room?"

*The dining room*, replied Primrose promptly. *So it will remind me of home.*

Zibby knelt in front of the dollhouse and reached

into the dining room. She centered the chandelier over the little mahogany table, then pressed the cardboard circle onto the ceiling. "I'm going to have to sit here for a while to hold it," she told Laura-Jane.

"That's okay. I can wait."

After several minutes, Zibby withdrew her hand from the little dining room. The glue held. The tiny glass beads of the chandelier glittered above the table like a handful of diamonds.

*Oohh, it's perfect,* came Primrose's happy voice. *Though I do wish it really lit up.*

Primrose would never be satisfied, Zibby realized. She had been that sort of person and now she was that sort of ghost. Well, it was just too bad. "I'm glad you like it," she said brightly. "Now, Laura-Jane and I have to go downstairs and return my mom's wallet. You stay here and enjoy the chandelier."

*But wait!*

"What is it now?" asked Zibby impatiently.

"It sounds so weird to hear you talking like that," said Laura-Jane from the doorway. "When we're not touching, I mean. I know you must be hearing that voice, but I can hear only yours. It's like you're talking to yourself."

"Well, I'm not," said Zibby. She got to her feet and went to Laura-Jane, took her hand and pulled her back across the room to the dollhouse. "You might as well hear what she has to say, too. Now what's the trouble, Primrose?"

*I can't go in and enjoy the chandelier,* moaned Primrose. *Because of Miss Honeywell!*

"You should have thought of that before you in-sisted I hang the chandelier!" snapped Zibby, who had forgotten herself.

Laura-Jane's fingers trembled in Zibby's own. But she bravely spoke to the ghost for the first time. "Y-you mean it's like the d-door's locked and you can't get in?"

*No.* Primrose tried to explain to Laura-Jane. *I can go in — in fact, Miss Honeywell wants me to come inside. But if I do, she'll have power over me. Don't you see? We have to get her out! But now that Zibby's hung the chandelier, she'll never come out! She loves it, I know she does.* Primrose's little voice was like the wailing mewl of a distressed cat. Zibby put her hands over her ears but it did nothing to stop the voice. *It's up to you, Zibby! You have to help me!*

"Calm down, calm down," said Zibby. "First things first. But I'll be back and we'll try to think of some-thing. Until then — well, maybe you can just stay out-side the house and look in the window at the chandelier. Or something."

*Cruel, cruel,* moaned Primrose.

Zibby released Laura-Jane's hand and walked to the door. "Let's go down and get this over with."

When Zibby and Laura-Jane started downstairs, they met up with Nell and Ned just coming down the attic stairs after tucking Brady into bed. The adults looked at each other in some surprise when they saw the girls together. The looks of surprise deepened when Zibby announced, "Laura-Jane needs to talk to you, Mom. Right now."

"Please," whispered Laura-Jane, looking down at the step she was standing on.

Nell smiled at her stepdaughter, but her eyes were wary. "Well, all right. Shall we go into the other room, Laura-Jane? Do you want to talk to me alone?"

Laura-Jane shook her head, looking frightened. "No, no . . . " She took a deep breath and looked at Zibby for support.

"Downstairs will be fine," said Zibby firmly. "Ned has to hear this, too. Everyone's going to hear about it sooner or later."

Ned motioned the girls ahead of them with an exaggerated, gentlemanly flourish. "Lead the way then, ladies." He spoke in a light voice. "This all sounds exceedingly mysterious."

Nell and Ned followed the girls downstairs to the dining room. The four of them sat around the dining room table underneath the twin cut-glass chandeliers very much like the one now hanging in the dollhouse. Laura-Jane remained silent, looking down at the bare tabletop, until Zibby cleared her throat pointedly. Then Laura-Jane's head jerked up and she caught Zibby's eye. Zibby saw then that her stepsister was fighting for the strength to confess. She wondered then how much of Laura-Jane's behavior had been influenced by Miss Honeywell's malevolent presence.

199

Battling both her own anger and the evil urgings of a ghost would be more than many people could bear, and she felt an unwilling admiration for the younger girl's resolve. Confessing wouldn't be easy.

Zibby gave Laura-Jane a nod. *Go on*, she urged Laura-Jane silently. *Get it over with!*

Laura-Jane nodded resolutely, almost as if she'd heard Zibby's thoughts. She drew a deep breath and looked straight at Nell. "I have to tell you first before I say anything else," she began softly, "that I didn't mean to hurt you. I was mad at you and Dad, and I guess I wanted to stir things up. Cause trouble. Make things hard for you. I know it was really mean. But I never wanted anyone to get hurt, and that's the truth."

Ned drew a sharp breath and was about to speak, but Nell held up her hand to silence him. "All right," Nell said gently. "Thank you for telling me that. But what are you talking about?"

And then Laura-Jane blurted out the whole story — the words spilling out like water from a broken dam. She cried while she spoke, and had to stop several times to wipe her streaming eyes. She told them how she'd been angry about their decision to marry, knowing it would ruin forever the chances of her own parents getting back together. She told them how she'd met Todd in the restaurant and been drawn to him, how he had spent time with her when no one else seemed to want to, and how he had invited her confidences. He had confessed to her his own unhappiness

200

with his parents, and his longing to stop feeling helpless and take action. But his father was always gone on business trips, leaving Todd in the care of a housekeeper, and his mother had indeed run off to join a circus — and so Laura-Jane's stepmother, living right there in the same house, seemed an easier target. His idea was that they should play some mean tricks on Nell, and Laura-Jane had agreed. But somehow the tricks had gotten out of hand and Laura-Jane wanted no more of them. Yet Todd continued his attacks on Nell, and Laura-Jane grew frightened — both for Nell and for herself.

By the time Laura-Jane held out the black leather wallet to her stepmother, Nell and Zibby were in tears, too. Ned had his head buried in his hands, so no one could tell whether he, too, were tearful. But no one would have been surprised if he were. *The only one in our family not crying is Brady*, thought Zibby, wiping her eyes, *because he's fast asleep and knows nothing about any of this*. For a moment she envied the little boy his innocence. Then she realized that for the first time she had included Laura-Jane as family.

Nell got up and wandered into the kitchen, and the others sat unmoving, each locked in private thoughts. Zibby was grateful when her mom returned after a few minutes with a box of tissues and a large bowl of microwave popcorn. She placed both on the table. "I think I need lots of both of these," she said with a rueful smile. "Feel free to dig in."

201

Ned chuckled and reached out for her hand. He gave it a squeeze, then took a handful of popcorn. "That's my Nelly," he said in a husky voice. "Can't keep a good woman down for long. I'll be able to write an article for the paper now, making sure the public knows that it was Todd who put the soap in the food. We'll set DaisyCakes right back on its feet again — before those Ballantynes steal the show."

"I don't think the Ballantynes have ever been a real threat, Ned," Nell murmured.

"No," he agreed, looking sorrowfully at his daughter. "It seems the real threat was much closer to home."

Zibby took some popcorn. Laura-Jane did not. She sat with her head bowed, twin ponytails dangling over her shoulders, cheeks flushed with shame.

Then they talked about why Laura-Jane had done it, and what should happen to her now. Ned, angry at his daughter and protective of Nell, suggested that maybe Laura-Jane would be happier if she went back to her mother in Fennel Grove. But Nell objected and said that if Laura-Jane were willing to make a fresh start, she should definitely have that chance. And Laura-Jane raised her head and smiled tremulously and said she would like to stay, as planned, until school started.

They talked about what would happen to Todd Parkfield, agreeing that a juvenile detention center was a possibility. But Nell said she was sorry about that, that reform school often made children tougher than when they went in. "It would be better if his parents could spend more time with him," she said. "I think he needs their support. His behavior is a cry for help."

Ned snorted that she was far too soft, and Laura-Jane reminded them in a murmur that Todd's mother was touring Europe with a circus under a five-year contract, and his father was about to accept a job in South America for six months.

"Well, he'll have to change his plans now, won't he?" Zibby said with asperity. Like Ned, she didn't feel sorry for Todd, though she knew it was just possible that he, too, had been one of Miss Honeywell's tools. "He'll need to be home to bail his son out of jail."

"Which reminds me," said Ned sternly, placing one heavy hand on Laura-Jane's shoulder. "You have a telephone call to make, young lady." And then he and Laura-Jane went off into the kitchen together to call the police.

Zibby and her mother looked at each other across the dining room table. "What a day, hmm?" said Nell, her shoulders drooping dispiritedly. She pushed the bowl of popcorn away and propped her head in her hands, elbows on the polished tabletop. "I don't think I can stand any more days like this one. I feel like the top of my head is coming off." She clutched her temples.

Zibby blinked. Her mom's headaches proved that not all the troubles Nell had been encountering could be laid at Todd's and Laura-Jane's door. "Poor you," she said with sympathy. "Will a head rub help?"

Nell nodded gratefully and closed her eyes. Zibby pushed back her chair and moved to stand behind her mom. She kneaded Nell's shoulders and neck, then inched her fingers up to massage Nell's head. Nell laid her head down on her crossed arms and moaned softly. Under Zibby's hands, her mom's red-gold hair felt soft and limp. She rubbed rhythmically, starting off gently and then pressing harder and harder.

Soon Ned and Laura-Jane returned from the kitchen. They walked into the dining room, Ned looking somber, Laura-Jane looking relieved. And because Nell's eyes were closed, she missed seeing what the three others saw: One of the two chandeliers — the one hanging from the ceiling almost directly above Nell's bent head — began to sway. It trembled for a moment as if set in motion by its own private earthquake, then slowly began to swing back and forth with a tinkling of glass pendants. Zibby, Laura-Jane, and Ned all gazed upward in horrified fascination.

"What's making it do that?" whispered Laura-Jane, hands pressed against her cheeks. Zibby released her mom's head and stood, openmouthed, as Ned grabbed a chair and jumped up on it to try to grab hold of the chandelier.

"Don't stop, Zib," murmured Nell in a sleepy voice. "That was so wonderful . . . " She opened her eyes and smiled, but the smile changed to a look of terror as she looked up just in time to see the nearest chandelier shake loose from the ceiling. In a flash, Zibby tackled her mom sideways, knocking her off her chair to the floor and landing on top of her just as the chandelier crashed down onto the table — right onto the place mat where Nell had laid her head. Sharp shards of glittering glass sliced into the air, and the heavy chain shattered the popcorn bowl and sent fluffy white kernels bouncing onto the floor.

In the shocked silence that followed, as Nell groaned and shifted under Zibby's weight, Zibby knew the danger to her mom was not over. It seemed that Laura-Jane was contrite for her part in all the trouble, and Todd would soon be in police custody — a threat to no one but himself. But cruel Miss Honeywell still meant business.

# Chapter 18

Ned put his arms around Nell and helped her to her feet. She kept her head buried on his shoulder, moaning that her migraine was making her see things. "No, we saw it, too," Ned said. "But only God knows what was going on. I've never seen anything like it in my life —" he broke off, lips pressed together.

"It was as if the house were haunted!" cried Nell. "Oh, Ned, what's going on? We've never had anything like this happen before. And I've lived in this house for years and years. Why should there suddenly be a ghost?" She groaned again and pressed her hands against her head. "I don't even believe in ghosts."

"Nor do I. There must be some other explanation."

Zibby and Laura-Jane stared at each other wordlessly. This would be the time, Zibby knew, to tell the adults about Miss Honeywell and have them believe her. But somehow she couldn't bring herself to explain.

"Like what?" pressed Nell. "Oh, Ned, what could have caused it?"

He shook his head. "An earthquake?" he asked doubtfully. "Something wrong with the wiring?"

"I've got to lie down before I fall down." She laughed shakily, without amusement. "Zibby, I think you probably saved my life — or at least saved me from being cut to ribbons. Thank you, darling."

"It's lucky you were right there, Zibby," Ned said. He glanced at his daughter. "We'll have to talk a lot more about all you told us tonight, Laura-Jane — but not tonight. At least the police are informed about Todd Parkfield now, and they'll deal with him." He glanced up at the cord from the broken chandelier and tightened his arm around Nell's shoulders. "Let me help you upstairs."

They walked slowly from the room, stepping over the shards of glass.

Laura-Jane sank onto a chair. "That was amazing. Was it really Miss Honeywell?"

"You know it was." Zibby went to the kitchen and came back with the dustpan and broom. "Come on — we'd better get this mess cleaned up before something else happens."

"Is something else going to happen?" asked Laura-Jane in her hushed voice. "I don't know what to be more afraid of — another ghost attack, or my dad. I'll probably get sent off to some boarding school now. It'll be as bad as reform school."

"Oh, I don't think so," said Zibby, starting to sweep up the glass while Laura-Jane held the dustpan. "I mean, I don't think he's thinking of boarding school. He's probably proud of you, for coming clean and telling the truth. At least, I know my mom and dad would be, if I did something like you did."

Laura-Jane sniffed and edged a piece of glass into the dustpan with one finger. "I can't imagine perfect old you ever doing something mean and nasty."

Zibby shrugged. "I guess I haven't, yet. But who knows? I hope at least I won't let myself be influenced by a creep like Todd Parkfield."

"But you liked him, too. I know you did."

"Well," she admitted, "I was starting to." And maybe that was one of the reasons her anger at him was so much greater than at Laura-Jane, Zibby realized. She had never liked Laura-Jane, but she'd liked Todd, and she'd trusted him. His betrayal seemed all the greater because of that.

"Anyway," she said now as they threw the broken glass away in the trash bin, "at least we know now what we're up against. That was Miss Honeywell's way of showing she's still here, and she's still out to get my mom. She has to do all the dirty work herself, now that Todd's out of the picture and you're not going to help her anymore."

Laura-Jane stared at her. "Do you mean you think Todd and I were, you know, possessed or something? That Miss Honeywell was making us do all that stuff?"

"Not exactly. You wanted to do it — it's not like Miss Honeywell took over your minds or anything."

Zibby remembered the flashes of gray skirt she'd thought she'd seen out of the corner of her eye. "But she may have made use of your willingness. I don't know." Zibby shook her head. "Poor Mom — she's had Todd and you and Miss Honeywell out to get her all at one time."

Laura-Jane flushed. "Well, at least Todd is out of the way, and I'm ready to help you get rid of Miss Honeywell." She twirled a loose strand of hair around her finger, biting her lower lip. "It's mostly my fault Miss Honeywell is on the warpath, right? So I owe your mom that — at the very least."

Zibby regarded her doubtfully. It was going to be hard for her to get used to a stepsister who wanted to be helpful and friendly, a stepsister who was remorseful and determined to make amends. It would mean she was going to have to spend time with Laura-Jane instead of ignoring her. It would mean she was going to have to treat her as a real sister instead of as an interloper.

It would mean more changes. But probably they'd be changes for the better. Things couldn't get much worse, after all.

Or could they? With Miss Honeywell, anything seemed possible.

"Okay," said Zibby. "Tomorrow morning we'll go tell the other girls about what's happened. Then — "

"Tell them *everything*?" interrupted Laura-Jane in a small voice.

Zibby frowned at her. "I don't hide things from my friends. And anyway, they already know most of it, don't they?"

Laura-Jane sighed. "It's just hard," she whispered. "I already feel so ashamed. Don't rub it in."

"I'm not rubbing it in!" said Zibby. "But I'm not going to lie about it, either. The important thing is that you're sorry, and you're going to help us get rid of Miss Honeywell, right?" When Laura-Jane nodded, Zibby smiled. "I'm hoping Primrose will help us, too. She hates Miss Honeywell even more than we do. So tomorrow we'll talk to the others and come up with a plan."

"Count me in," said Laura-Jane.

In the morning Zibby and Laura-Jane got up at the same time and went down to eat breakfast. They found Ned in the kitchen, scribbling a note on the pad by the telephone. "Oh, there you are," he greeted them. "I'm off to work now to write up an article about earthquakes in Carroway. But I was just leaving you a message."

"What message?" asked Laura-Jane nervously. She was worried, Zibby knew, about how her dad would be "dealing" with her, as he'd put it the night before.

"Just that Nell is still in bed with a pounding head, and not feeling great. I don't want anyone to bother her. I'd like you two to look after Brady — keep him out of her way until she's feeling better. If he wants to

210

go out and play with friends, that's fine, and it's fine if you two go out, too, as long as you take him with you or tell him where you're going." Ned turned to his daughter and placed his hands heavily on her shoulders. "You, I'd like to see at the newspaper office at noon. We're going out to lunch."

"We are?" whispered Laura-Jane.

"Don't be late. And Zibby? Please make sure you're home at noon so you can get lunch for yourself and for Brady if your mom isn't up and about yet. Okay?"

"Okay," nodded Zibby.

After Ned had gone, Laura-Jane and Zibby sat eating cereal and musing about why Ned was taking her to lunch. "It's not much of a punishment, really," said Laura-Jane. "He can't yell at me in a restaurant!"

"He probably just wants to talk things over," said Zibby. "That's what my dad would do." For a moment she missed her dad fiercely. She wanted to go out to lunch with him.

"I keep forgetting you have a father," said Laura-Jane, then looked down at her cereal when Zibby frowned at her.

After a while Brady came zooming into the room, half-dressed. The girls sent him back to find his T-shirt. They ate breakfast quickly. Brady sat with them, flicking Cheerios across the table at the carton of milk and shouting "Goal!" whenever one hit, which was nearly every one. Zibby winced and moved the carton of milk to the counter by the sink. "Hold it down,

Brady," she said. "My mom is still sleeping, and she has a terrible headache again."

Only a day or so ago, Laura-Jane might have smiled with satisfaction at Zibby's words, and maybe even urged her brother on to louder and wilder games. But now she nodded seriously and said, "And if you're going to watch cartoons this morning, keep the volume down, too."

"I'm not going to watch TV! Me and James and Melissa are going to the moon." Brady grabbed the last cinnamon bun. "They said I should come over early so we could get started building our rocket." He frowned. "I hope Todd won't be mad at me, but I've decided I'm not going to be an alpha — no, an *acrobat* after all. I'm going to be an acronaut!"

"You mean an *astronaut*," Zibby corrected him patiently.

"That's what I said. We're going to fly to the moon first, and then go to Jupiter!"

"Well, just make sure you look both ways before you cross the street," Laura-Jane warned as Brady careened out of the room. In a moment they heard the slam of the screen door.

Zibby and Laura-Jane looked at each other and shrugged. "I know he's kind of crazy," Laura-Jane said fondly, walking to the window and looking out at where her little brother was standing at the curb, looking back and forth for cars along the quiet street. "But he's a sweet kid."

"I think so, too," said Zibby. "I just have to get used to having him around, that's all."

"He is sort of loud," Laura-Jane agreed.

"Maybe that's why you're so quiet." Zibby glanced at her watch. It was only nine o'clock, but she knew Jude and Penny would be awake. She'd better phone Charlotte, though, to make sure she was out of bed and ready to meet at the clubhouse tree.

"I didn't know I was so quiet," whispered Laura-Jane.

Zibby pushed her hair back in exasperation.

The five girls sat on the low branches of the leafy clubhouse. Penny was scuffing her sandals in the grass. Jude was studying the veins of a leaf. Both were managing to conceal their amazement at Laura-Jane's presence. Only Charlotte was not so tactful. She nudged Zibby, sitting next to her on the branch, and hissed: "What did you bring *her* here for?"

Of course Laura-Jane heard this, and ducked her head. Her twin ponytails swung forward to hide the flush of her cheeks.

"There's a lot to tell you," Zibby said defensively. "And Laura-Jane is part of it. I said she should come and tell you herself, and so that's why she's here." She glared around at the other girls. "Any objections?"

"Nope," said Jude readily. "I never said a word, did I?"

"Not exactly," admitted Zibby. "But nobody seems very, you know, *welcoming*."

Generous Penny looked up with a smile and stopped scuffing her feet. "Of course it's fine that you're here, Laura-Jane. What did you want to tell us?"

Laura-Jane cleared her throat. "It's about — Miss Honeywell." Her voice came out so softly the others had to strain to hear. "She's still trying to hurt Nell."

"That's right," said Zibby. "And we need to stop her before she can do any more damage." Quickly she told the others about how the swinging chandelier came crashing down on the table, narrowly missing her mom's head. "We've got to think fast."

"Well," said Jude after the exclamations died down. "Five heads ought to be better than one — or two," she added, glancing at Laura-Jane. "With all of us working on it, we ought to be able to come up with a plan that works."

Zibby looked at her friend gratefully. She could count on Jude to be nice to Laura-Jane once the shock of seeing her here in the clubhouse had worn off. And Penny was nice to just about everybody anyway. It was Charlotte she wasn't so sure about.

Well, Laura-Jane had it coming to her, in a way, she reflected. Her stepsister would have to make some effort to stand up for herself if she was going to hang out with the others. She would talk to them later about Laura-Jane, and try to explain why she was now willing to include her stepsister. How the hatred and anger had all but disappeared when she'd found Laura-Jane practicing her confession with the dollhouse dolls.

214

How Laura-Jane's tearful talk with Nell and Ned, and her real remorse had melted much of the ice around Zibby's heart. How she'd come to believe that maybe Laura-Jane had a good side after all. How maybe her attraction to Todd Parkfield had been in response to a need for a friend. She'd chosen badly. But maybe she could do better if she felt included in Zibby's group of friends.

But now they had more pressing things to talk about.

"The problem with Miss Honeywell is that we don't know what she wants," mused Jude. "We've never really known that — even when you first bought the haunted dollhouse, Zibby, and discovered her there. Why doesn't she just go on to — heaven? Or wherever it is that mean governesses go when they're dead?"

"Maybe she's not welcome in heaven," said Charlotte with a sly smile. "No halo for Old Honeywell!" She looked over at Laura-Jane and spoke in an innocent-sounding voice. "People who do bad things don't get halos, Laura-Jane. Did you know that?"

"Oh, shut up, Char," said Penny. "That's not very nice."

"Well, it's probably true. Miss Honeywell was a little kid once, too, remember. And she probably was doing mean things even back then. When she grew up, she got meaner." Charlotte smirked at Laura-Jane. "It happens, you know."

"Well, Laura-Jane isn't like that." Zibby spoke up in

215

defense of her stepsister, who stood up and pushed out of the bower of leaves with a sob. Zibby jumped up and followed her out, grabbing her arm as she tried to run off across the grass.

"Come on, Laura-Jane. Don't leave. Charlotte's got a mean streak, too, you know. I could tell you stories! She's not a prime candidate for a halo either, believe me!"

"I want to go home," Laura-Jane said in an agonized whisper. "Let go of me, Zibby!"

"No! I want you to stay here. We need your ideas." She put her face close to Laura-Jane's. "Charlotte can be a pain, but remember, you haven't been very nice to anybody. Why not stay and show them the real you?"

"The *real* me?" Laura-Jane searched Zibby's face. "I think the real me disappeared when my real family did. When my dad left home."

Zibby sighed. "I think I know what you mean. It happened to me, too. But I don't think it was the real me who disappeared. It was just one version. Now I'm a different version. If my dad still lived with us, I wouldn't know you and Ned and Brady. And maybe I'd know nothing about ghosts, and we wouldn't have this club to figure out how to deal with them, and my life would be totally different. I'm not so sure I'd want that. Would you?"

Laura-Jane smiled hesitantly. "Well, maybe not. But I bet your mom wouldn't be in danger if your dad still lived with you."

216

"No," Zibby agreed thoughtfully. "But I'm not so sure she'd be happy, even so. She really loves your dad. She told me she's loved him since they were in high school."

Before Laura-Jane had a chance to respond, Jude pushed her way out of the clubhouse and came over to stand on the grass with them. "Laura-Jane," she began earnestly. "We've been talking, and we're sorry we didn't act very, um, welcoming. Even Charlotte. And we hope you won't go home and will come back in and try to think of a plan with us." She waited. "Okay?"

"Oh — all right," said Laura-Jane, and it seemed to Zibby that her stepsister's voice was a little bit louder.

They ducked back under the leafy green branches. Penny looked up with a relieved smile, but Charlotte just sat studying her perfectly polished fingernails. When Penny nudged her, she flipped back her long hair and tried to look contrite.

Zibby and Laura-Jane resumed their seats. Laura-Jane stared at the ground.

"So, where were we?" asked Charlotte briskly. "We were saying how we don't really know what this nasty Old Honeywell wants, right?"

"We do know what she wants," said Zibby, settling herself back on her branch. "She wants power. Power over Primrose Parson, and over other kids."

"Ever the governess," added Charlotte.

"And she wants the house," cried Penny.

"And the chandelier!" said Jude. "She's greedy and

she likes fine things, right? And she never had any herself, really. Even though she lived in Primrose's grand house, nothing in it really belonged to her. She must have gone around green with jealousy all the time."

"I suppose," said Zibby slowly, "we could make her a house of her own." Zibby had received a tool set for her birthday, and she knew she could bang a house together quickly. "I'd have to work fast, but I could get it done if I had some wood — Jude, do you think maybe your grandfather could give us some wood from the lumberyard?"

Mr. Jefferson, who was Jude's grandfather and Penny's father, owned the big lumberyard on the road between Carroway and Fennel Grove.

"I'm sure he would," replied Jude. "But you couldn't make as nice a dollhouse as the one you've already got — not quickly, anyway. And as we've just been saying, Miss Honeywell likes fine things. She'd never get lured into something ramshackle."

"I could make something better than ramshackle!" Zibby objected.

"But I see what you mean," said Charlotte. "*My* dollhouse is elegant enough — but I don't want Miss Honeywell living anywhere near me."

Zibby shot her cousin a withering look. "Some cousin *you* are!"

Penny, ever the peacemaker, spoke up hastily. "How about if we all pool our money and buy Miss Honeywell a new dollhouse?" she asked. "I have eleven dollars. We could go to that miniature shop in Fennel Grove."

"But really elegant houses cost a lot more than we can afford," said Zibby.

The girls fell silent. Penny started scuffing her feet in the grass again. Charlotte inspected her painted nails. Jude and Zibby looked at each other hopelessly.

Then Laura-Jane spoke up for the first time since she'd returned to the clubhouse. "I've got it," she said, and her voice came out not a whisper but low and firm. "We can give Miss Honeywell *my* dollhouse. It's big and, well, very pink and ugly. But if we pooled our money like Penny suggested, we could buy some nice furniture that Miss Honeywell would want."

"That would be perfect," said Jude warmly.

"Yeah," agreed Charlotte. "And it's a good thing the dollhouse is already at your house, so Miss Honeywell won't have to move very far."

"You are *so* generous, Charlotte." Zibby made a face at her cousin.

Charlotte raised her brows in a superior expression. "What if your face froze that way?"

"Stop fighting!" sighed Penny.

"Does the house close up and lock?" asked Zibby. "It can't be one of those usual houses with the open back because then we can't keep the ghost inside."

"It does lock," Laura-Jane told her. "It's a big boxy thing and opens on hinges. It latches closed with plastic fasteners — you've seen it, Zibby."

"But I never looked at it closely." Zibby had never been in Laura-Jane's room for long enough to be introduced to her stepsister's books or toys or clothes, but this wasn't the time to remind Laura-Jane of that.

"Miss Honeywell might not like such a pink palace," Charlotte pointed out.

Penny frowned, thinking. "We'll have to furnish it with things the other house doesn't have. So she can feel superior to Primrose."

"Good thinking, Aunt Penny," Jude said solemnly.

"Don't you dare call me *Aunt* — " began Penny crossly, but Charlotte interrupted.

"What can we lure her out with?" she asked. "It'll have to be something she really wants."

Zibby tipped her head up and studied the green leaves overhead. She reached up idly and pulled one off, rubbing its smooth shape between her fingers. She thought about Primrose, stuck outside, longing to go back into her dollhouse. She thought about Miss Honeywell, unseen and unheard but menacing, tucked away in the dollhouse, enjoying the fine art on the walls and the new chandelier . . .

"I know," Zibby said suddenly, throwing the leaf to the ground as if it were a gauntlet and she were a knight ready to meet the challenge. "The chandelier! Miss Honeywell knows how much Primrose wants it. So we'll move it to the pink house and she'll move in after it!"

"Primrose will be furious," predicted Penny, looking worried.

"Too bad for Primrose," said Jude, getting to her feet and brushing off the seat of her jeans. "At least she'll have her house back, and Miss Honeywell will be locked up where she can't do any more damage."

"So what are we waiting for?" cried Laura-Jane in a voice that was not by any stretch of the imagination a whisper, but loud and clear and ringing with excitement. "Let's go!"

# Chapter 19

The five girls hurried down the street to Zibby's — and now Laura-Jane's—house. They raced up the stairs to Laura-Jane's attic bedroom. Nell's faint voice called to them from the master bedroom where she was still lying in bed.

"Zibby? Laura-Jane?" Nell moaned. "Keep the noise down. Even the tiniest noise sounds like thunder."

"Sorry, Mom," Zibby said, pausing on the stairs. The girls continued up to Laura-Jane's room on tiptoe.

Brady and his friends from across the street popped out of his bedroom to see what was going on.

"Nell said we could play up here if we were very quiet," he told his sister defensively. "And we are being quiet. We're drawing maps of outer space to take on our journey. Right, guys?"

The other little boy and girl nodded solemnly. Laura-Jane shrugged. "I never said you couldn't play up here," she said mildly.

"Well, you looked mad, like you were *about* to say something!" Brady insisted.

"Laura-Jane's just worried about my mom," Zibby told him soothingly. "That's why she's looking so gloomy." She had to smile at herself — standing up for Laura-Jane wasn't something she was used to doing.

"Come on," urged Charlotte.

"We have work to do," added Jude. "And fast."

The little kids disappeared back into Brady's room and shut the door. Penny beckoned the girls into Laura-Jane's room. She was already over by the pink dollhouse, inspecting it. "I think this will work," she said. "Even though it's not a really grand kind of house. It does stand out in a crowd!"

"You can say that again," Charlotte said, looking with distaste at the garish pink plastic. "But maybe that will appeal to somebody like Miss Honeywell. Who knows? I just hate to waste that gorgeous chandelier on a dump like this."

"I didn't choose this house, you know," Laura-Jane muttered. "It was a Christmas present from my aunt when I was about Brady's age."

"I never said you chose it!" returned Charlotte. "I just said it's ugly. And it is."

"Well I think it is, too!"

"Come on, come on," said Penny soothingly. "We have to carry the thing downstairs. Is it heavy?" She tried to pick it up. "Not really, but it's hard to hold on to!"

Zibby hurried to help her. She backed out of Laura-Jane's room with Penny holding the other side of the pink house. They maneuvered it into the hallway and slowly descended the stairs. Quietly, so as not to disturb Nell, they carried the house to Zibby's bedroom.

Charlotte, Jude, and Laura-Jane crept along behind, each of them carrying an armful of plastic dollhouse furniture. They dumped the lot of it onto Zibby's bed. Zibby and Penny carefully lowered the pink house onto the floor next to Zibby's antique dollhouse.

"Here, let me set up the rooms," said Penny eagerly. She started placing hard plastic beds and hard plastic dressers into the little plastic bedrooms.

"I'll help you." Laura-Jane grabbed the plastic couches and plastic dining table and placed them in the appropriate downstairs rooms.

Jude looked on with a dubious expression in her dark eyes. She fingered the little wooden beads at the ends of her long skinny braids, a habit she had when she was nervous or worried.

"What's wrong?" asked Zibby in a low voice.

"I'm thinking it's not going to work. Too much plastic. It's not so much the color pink — I mean, maybe Miss Honeywell will go for garish stuff. But it's the — well, the *hardness* of it all." She reached out and picked up a green plastic armchair. "I mean, look at this. Would you want to sit in it?"

"Or sleep in this?" added Charlotte, reaching into

the house and removing one of the beds Penny had just arranged. "The pillow and covers are just molded plastic. Miss Honeywell goes for comfort. Even a chandelier isn't going to be enough to lure her into a house where everything is ugly pink plastic."

"Either she moves in or she doesn't," said Penny. "It depends on how much she wants that chandelier, right?"

"Right," agreed Charlotte. "But it won't hurt to add a few nice blankets and pillows and things from the other dollhouse. Primrose doesn't need all those things."

"Okay," said Zibby. "Go ahead and make it as cozy for nasty Old Honeywell as you want. I'll take down the chandelier."

So Laura-Jane and Penny set up all the plastic furniture in the pink dollhouse while Jude and Charlotte pillaged the antique wooden dollhouse for things to make Miss Honeywell's new home more inviting. They took tiny pillows from the yellow bedroom and an embroidered quilt from the green bedroom. They took an upholstered chair from the drawing room, and two of the little stamp pictures in their colorful wooden frames. They even took some of the miniature silverware from the dining room. Zibby ran down to the kitchen and found a pretty paper cocktail napkin patterned with roses. This she trimmed into a circle, using the scissors from her desk, and then she laid it atop the pink plastic dining room table in the pink dollhouse. Jude set the table with the silverware, with one of Primrose's potted plants as a centerpiece.

"There!" said Zibby, pleased with the effect. "So now we only need the chandelier." She had carefully levered off the little cardboard circle that had been glued to the ceiling of the antique dollhouse. Now she took it over to her desk and dabbed glue onto the back of the cardboard.

She waited a minute until the glue became tacky, then she carefully pressed it into place on the ceiling of the pink plastic dining room. She waited — all the girls waited — counting slowly to one hundred. Then she let go and the chandelier dangled over the plastic table set with tablecloth, silverware, and potted plant. The chandelier transformed the little pink room. Its glittering glass stones sparkled in the light.

*Oh, woe is me!* moaned Primrose's sorrowful voice faintly in Zibby's head. *I waited so long for that chandelier, only to have it snatched away again. Why are you doing this to torment me, Zibby? Do you want me to move into the other house?*

"No! Not you, Primrose," whispered Zibby.

"Is she complaining again?" asked Jude. "Here, let me talk to her." She put her hand in Zibby's and spoke. "Primrose Parson? You just sit tight and don't do anything. Don't go *anywhere*. We're trying to help you, don't you understand that? But in order to help you, we need the chandelier. You can't have everything."

*Well, I don't see why not,* chirped the ghost.

226

Jude and Zibby sighed.

"Look!" Penny's excited shout made them all jump. The other girls rushed to look where she was pointing. "I think it's working!"

The newly installed chandelier, now hanging over the table in the pink plastic house, was moving. It was swinging gently back and forth, back and forth, just as the real one had the night before in the real dining room downstairs in Zibby's house. Zibby drew in her breath as the tiny chandelier began to swing in a circle.

Charlotte backed away and sank onto the bed. Laura-Jane covered her mouth with her hands in fright.

"She's in there," Zibby whispered. "Quick! Close it up!"

She and Jude reached out at the same time and slammed the front of the pink plastic house. The house seemed to heave under their hands, bucking and shaking as the force within it struggled to get out. "Laura-Jane!" cried Zibby. "How do you lock this thing?"

Laura-Jane edged forward, her eyes dark with fear. She pressed the plastic latches closed with trembling fingers, then drew back as if she'd received an electric shock. "Can't ghosts go through walls?" she asked in an agonized whisper.

"Not dollhouse walls, somehow," said Zibby.

The girls kept well away while the tightly locked pink plastic house vibrated. Through the tiny windows they could see into the dining room. The silverware fell off the table and the little plant tumbled around the floor as the house heaved. The chandelier overhead continued to swing. It swung around more and more wildly on its thin threads, arcing into the air and swirling in a mad gypsy dance. And then they heard the tinkle of glass as the threads broke and the jewel-like beads danced across the plastic floor.

From down the hall they heard Nell's voice cry out — and then all was silent.

The pink house sat unmoving now on the rug, still safely locked. Zibby jumped to her feet and dashed out of the room. What had Miss Honeywell done to her mom now?

But she nearly collided with Nell in the hallway. "Oh, Mom!" Zibby cried. "What's wrong? I heard you cry — "

"It was incredible, Zibby," Nell said faintly, but there was a smile on her lips. "The pain was all of a sudden the worst I've ever felt. I thought my head was about to come off. I screamed — and then just as suddenly it was gone. Completely gone. In fact, I feel fine. Better than I have — well, since before the wedding. It's amazing." Nell touched her head tentatively, checking for pain and finding none. "I'm just going to take a shower now and I'll feel one-hundred percent human again." She laughed. "What a relief!" Then she looked at Zibby's pale face with concern. "Are *you* all right, honey?"

"Yes," said Zibby. "At least, I think so." She slipped

back inside her own room to find the four other girls sitting motionless around the pink house.

"Better come look at this, Zib," whispered Jude. "You're not going to believe it."

What now?

Holding her breath, Zibby moved forward and knelt between Jude and Laura-Jane on the rug. Charlotte, her blue eyes round with shock, pointed a finger at the dining room window.

Zibby leaned to look inside the pink house. And there she saw the governess doll — wearing her long gray skirt — sitting at the little plastic table in a little plastic chair.

"Where did that come from?" she demanded. "Who put it inside?"

The other girls just shook their heads. It was Primrose Parson's little voice, piping up in a whine inside Zibby's head that supplied the answer.

*She just appeared, Zibby. But that's good, isn't it? Miss Honeywell is locked up. And that means I can go home now, doesn't it?*

"Yeah," breathed Zibby. Fear tickled her spine as she looked in at the motionless doll in the pink house. *As long as she stays locked up,* Zibby thought fiercely, *we'll be all right.*

"What do we do now?" whispered Laura-Jane.

"We take this house down to the basement," Zibby said decisively. "Unless you want it in your bedroom."

"Are you kidding!" shrieked Laura-Jane. "I never want to see it again!"

"I doubt we'll be so lucky," said Jude, peering in again at the still figure of the doll. "But at least the house locks up tight."

"And so does the basement," added Zibby. The two friends exchanged a long look. Neither really believed anymore — if indeed they ever had — that ghosts could be contained by locks. At least not for long. Too much had happened for that.

The girls trundled the pink house down into the hallway. Nell, entering the bathroom for her shower, looked at them in surprise.

"I don't want this in my room," Laura-Jane explained quickly. "It's — um, too pink."

"Well, there's space in the corner by the furnace," Nell said. "Put it there."

They put it there and left it. *I hope the spiders get busy fast*, Zibby thought. She didn't want to see it again.

When they returned to Zibby's room, the late summer's afternoon sun slanted across the room and highlighted the antique house as if with a spotlight.

Zibby peeked into the house. The little girl doll in the blue dress sat at the elegant dining table just as the governess doll did in the pink house. The table was beautifully set with Primrose's remaining silverware and little china plates. It was set for six.

*There's a place for each of you girls,* came Primrose's

flutey little voice inside Zibby's head. *There won't be any real food, of course. But we can pretend, can't we?*

"Sure," said Zibby with a smile. The other girls reached out to hold hands so they, too, could hear the ghost.

*I wanted to serve you a banquet, to thank you for all you have done,* Primrose continued. *Imagine a lovely chocolate cake and fruit ice cream and jam rolls. Imagine fizzy drinks and pink lemonade!*

The girls looked at each other, then back into the dining room. Primrose's voice took on its familiar whine. *Of course it would be so much more elegant if there were a chandelier in here,* she said petulantly. *How can I invite you to an elegant afternoon tea with no chandelier?*

But Zibby had had enough of chandeliers to last a lifetime. "We'll have to pretend about that, too," she told the ghost firmly.

# Chapter 20

Zibby woke to a cool breeze flowing through her open window. She snuggled beneath her cotton blanket and thought it wouldn't be much longer before they'd have to unpack the heavy warm quilts put away for the hot summer months.

Funny to think that school would start in only a week. So much had happened since fifth grade ended! Then Zibby'd been crushed that her best friend, Amy, had moved away. She was expecting to have a miserably boring summer with only her snooty cousin Charlotte for company.

At the beginning of the summer she hadn't known Ned Shimizu. She'd never heard of Laura-Jane and Brady. And now her mom had remarried her high-school sweetheart, and Laura-Jane and Brady were her stepsister and stepbrother.

She'd had her eleventh birthday. She'd met Jude and Penny. She'd bought the antique dollhouse at the miniature show and embarked on the strangest and most terrifying adventures of her life. She'd never believed in ghosts before. Now she lived with two of them.

The summer had turned out to be anything but *boring*.

And she lived with the newfound knowledge that first impressions couldn't always be trusted. Handsome, charming Todd Parkfield had turned out to be a very unpleasant character. And Hilda and Hector Ballantyne, two of the most sour-faced, rude people Zibby had ever met were not the criminals she had suspected them to be. Laura-Jane was turning out to have an approachable side, though Zibby couldn't really consider Laura-Jane a friend, nor yet a real sister. But there would be time to work on that.

Zibby stretched and sat up in bed. For the first time in what seemed like ages there was no urgent need to jump out of bed. No preparations for the wedding, no need to keep watch over her mom's safety, no club meetings scheduled to figure out how to unmask the attacker or to deal with Miss Honeywell. She could lie here all day if she wanted.

But she didn't want to. The summer was fading away all too quickly. Zibby was looking forward to catching up during the next couple of days on some of the things she'd meant to do but hadn't done all summer.

Like lying in the back garden, reading. Like writing a long cheerful letter to her dad asking him to teach her Italian through the mail. Like phoning Amy to see if she could come to visit again. Like going to the pool and hanging out with some of the school kids. She could take Jude and Penny along and introduce them, too. Jude and Penny had been such a part of Zibby's life this summer, she sometimes forgot they'd only just moved to Carroway in June. They could get Charlotte — and, okay, even Laura-Jane — and ride bikes along the river . . .

*And what about me?* came the voice of Primrose Parson in Zibby's head.

Zibby shook back her red-gold hair vigorously, as if doing so would shake the ghostly voice right out of her head.

*Zibby!* came the voice again when Zibby didn't answer. It held a wheedling tone that made Zibby's guard go up.

"What is it, Primrose?" she asked warily. Couldn't she even plan a day out with her friends without ghosts intruding? Would she be reminded of ghosts every single day of her life?

*Do you know what I've been thinking about, here in my gloomy, dark old house?*

"What, Primrose?" asked Zibby obediently. "Not a chandelier, I hope."

*No, I've been thinking that what I need now is a conservatory. How about it, child? You're supposed to be a good carpenter, aren't you? Though in my day that was no fitting occupation for a girl! I should say not! But I do so long for a conservatory and —*

234

"No." Zibby didn't have the faintest idea what a conservatory was, and she didn't want to know. "I need a vacation, Primrose."

She pushed off her blanket and swung her legs over the side of the bed.

*But we had one when I was a girl. All the finest homes had one. It was a glass room built onto the house — rather like a greenhouse, Zibby. It was a whole paradise for plants. But there was furniture, too. White wicker rockers and little tables for afternoon tea parties . . .*

"No!" Zibby crossed to her dresser and pulled out some clean clothes. It was cool enough now for jeans rather than shorts. She put on a long-sleeved T-shirt, too, then headed out the door.

*Just one little conservatory, that's all I'm asking!* Primrose's nagging voice accompanied Zibby down the stairs to the kitchen. *If you build one for me I'll never ask for anything else.*

"That'll be the day," muttered Zibby.

Laura-Jane, seated at the breakfast table, set her glass of orange juice down in surprise and stared at Zibby. "What'll be the day?"

"It's Primrose," Zibby told her in a low voice, glancing around to make sure her mom, Ned, and Brady were out of earshot. "She wants a greenhouse. Can you believe it?"

Laura-Jane chuckled softly. "I think I can believe just about anything after what I saw — and heard — yesterday." She reached out and touched Zibby's arm with a shy smile.

*It's a conservatory, not a greenhouse,* Primrose's tiny voice corrected Zibby. *Since I don't have a chandelier. And speaking of chandeliers —*

Zibby looked at Laura-Jane. "See what I have to put up with?"

Laura-Jane moved away and reached for the orange juice carton. She poured some more into her own glass, then filled one for Zibby. "Well, now that I know what's going on, I can try to help you out with her." She glanced over at the door leading down to the basement. "If I don't die of fright first."

Both girls raised their glasses and opened their mouths to drink — then stopped at the sound of a thud beneath them. They lowered the glasses and stared at each other over the rims.

They strained their ears, listening. Could Miss Honeywell break out of her pink prison?

*Promise me you'll think about the conservatory,* wheedled Primrose Parson into their silence. *And a new chandelier.*

And slowly Zibby nodded. It wouldn't do to lose Primrose's goodwill — especially if Miss Honeywell might someday be back to haunt them. "All right," she agreed resolutely. "I'll think about them — *if* you don't say another word about them. For — a month! A whole month. Not one word."

She was learning you have to be firm with ghosts. They could be an awful pain, but Primrose, at least, had her good points, too. Zibby raised her glass of orange juice to Laura-Jane. The two girls clinked the glasses together across the kitchen table in a toast.

"To ghosts?" asked Laura-Jane.

"To ghosts," agreed Zibby, and Primrose's tinkling laughter filled her head.

# Dollhouse
# Furnishings
# You Can Make

Keeping Primrose Parson happy means that Zibby and her friends spend a lot of time crafting new items for the dollhouse. The craft projects are not hard to do, but they do need special care. You can make similar gifts for the inhabitants of your dollhouse, too!

## Framed Artwork

What you'll need:

small pictures cut from magazines,
small photographs, or postage stamps
glue or paste, scissors, and tape

239

thin cardboard
wooden matchsticks (snip off the heads),
toothpicks, or thin lengths of balsa wood
colored marking pens, crayons or paints

1. Glue the picture you want to frame onto a piece of thin cardboard and let it dry.
2. Then use scissors to trim the cardboard to the same size as the picture.
3. Fit the wooden sticks around the picture and trim them to size.
4. Then glue the sticks into place at the edges of the picture to make the frame.
5. When the wooden frame is dry, decorate it with markers.
6. Stick the framed picture onto the wall of your dollhouse with a little roll of tape.

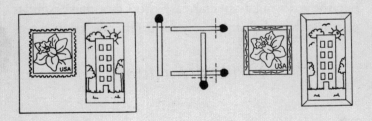

# Beaded Chandelier

What you'll need:
> a pair of beaded earrings for pierced ears
> a sewing needle thin enough to pass through the holes in the beads
> thread
> piece of thin cardboard
> scissors, tape, and glue

1. The easiest way to make a chandelier is simply to join the two earrings by twisting the wires together. If you would like to make your chandelier more elaborate, you may want to snip the beads apart and string them a different way (using the needle and thread).

2. Once your chandelier is formed, cut a circular shape from the cardboard, about one inch in diameter.

3. Poke a hole in the center of the cardboard circle, then push the earring wires through the hole. Make sure the beaded chandelier hangs down evenly from the cardboard, then tape the wires flat against the back of the cardboard circle.

4. Glue the cardboard circle to the ceiling of your dollhouse room. The chandelier should dangle beautifully. Chandeliers look especially nice hanging over the dining room table or in a hallway.

  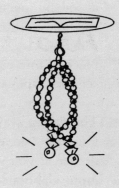

# About the Author

Kathryn Reiss has written numerous novels for young readers including *Time Windows* and *Dreadful Sorry,* which are both available as Scholastic paperbacks.

Ms. Reiss holds an MFA in creative writing from the University of Michigan. She lives in Oakland, California, with her husband, two sons, and daughter.

Don't miss

# THE GHOST IN THE DOLLHOUSE

## *Rest in Peace # 3*

Zibby closed her eyes. In seconds sleep overcame her. But it was not the light, refreshing sleep of an ordinary midday nap. This sleep was deep and still. Zibby felt herself being sucked down into quiet, almost as if she were being pulled under water. Sleep wrapped itself around her, anchoring her with a heavy, unmoving weight.

Sometime later she heard a crackling sound and opened her eyes in confusion. She fought her way out of the deep, muffling sleep and sat up in bed in alarm, seeing — then smelling — the smoke billowing through her bedroom. She coughed and tried to see through the gray haze. She could make out orange flames leaping toward the ceiling.

Her dollhouse was on fire.

Zibby leaped from her bed and started for the door, looking back over her shoulder at the fire, trying to remember what to do. Keep low; the air is fresher near the floor. Warn the family and get out of the house fast. Run next door and phone for the firefighters. . . . But she stopped as if frozen when she saw something move in the blaze.

It was a hand.

Enter the dollhouse.
Play at your own risk.

# THE GHOST IN THE DOLLHOUSE

## Book #1: Dollhouse of the Dead
## by Kathryn Reiss

Zibby never wanted the shabby, old
dollhouse. But something called out
to her. When she gets it home, things
start to get weird. She tries to get rid
of it—but it always ends up back in
its place. Now Zibby is really scared.
What does the dollhouse want?

**The terror continues:**
Book #2: The Headless Bride...Coming in April
Book #3: Rest in Peace...Coming in May

## Soon to haunt a bookstore near you!